IN or OUT

BY CLAUDIA GABEL

IN or OUT

LOVES ME, LOVES ME NOT
An IN or OUT Novel

IN or OUT

A novel by

CLAUDIA GABEL

SCHOLASTIC INC.

New York   Toronto   London   Auckland   Sydney   Mexico City   New Delhi   Hong Kong   Buenos Aires

ISBN-13: 978-0-545-03802-7
ISBN-10: 0-545-03802-2

Text design by Steve Scott
The text type was set in Iowan Old Style.

12 11 10 9 8 7 6 5 4 3 2 1   7 8 9 10 11 12/0

Printed in the U.S.A.
This edition first printing, September 2007

For Therese — LYLAS.

Chapter 1

It was the last day of summer, but to Nola James, the sun felt as strong as it had in the beginning of June. She'd been out in her Poughkeepsie, New York, backyard all Wednesday afternoon and now she could feel her skin sizzling. Nola loved quiet summer moments like this, when she could stretch out on a deck chair in her favorite blue-and-white-striped bikini, close her eyes, and forget all her worries.

But today, Nola's worries wouldn't disappear, no matter how long she worshipped the sun.

"I feel like a rotisserie chicken," moaned her best friend, Marnie Fitzpatrick, from the deck chair beside Nola. Blonde-haired and fair-skinned, Marnie usually preferred the shade of her dad's giant golf umbrella.

"This was your idea, remember? You said you didn't want to start school looking all pale." Nola's stomach jumped the second she said the word *school*. Wasn't she a little too old for all this nervousness?

Marnie sat up and took a sip from the yellow plastic glass that was resting on the arm of her chair. "I know, I know. It's just *so* hot out. Maybe we should give up." She blotted her glistening freckled face with a purple beach towel. "Do you think City Drug carries tan-in-a-can?"

"Probably." Nola retied her long, light brown hair into a sloppy knot on top of her head. "Just try not to turn Jessica Simpson–orange, like you did on the Fourth of July."

"I happen to like orange, okay?" Marnie threw her towel at Nola and smiled.

Nola knew this was a lie. Actually, she pretty much knew everything about Marnie. For instance: her favorite movie (*The 40-Year-Old Virgin*), her least favorite brand of jeans (Joe's), and her most embarrassing moment (she had spit out a mouthful of chai shake at Häagen-Dazs last month after Patrick Callahan, who held the number six spot on her Crush List, told her a funny joke).

Marnie knew a million little secrets about Nola, too. The girls had met in kindergarten, and Nola had turned Marnie into her honorary sister.

In fact, Nola and Marnie signed every correspondence between them — whether it was an e-mail or an old-fashioned folded-up note — with *LYLAS*, which was shorthand for Love Ya Like A Sister. Over the years, the girls had established traditions, like their Friday night movie-sleepovers and their very anticlimactic bumper bowling competitions on the last Saturday of every month. But tomorrow Nola would be surrounded by hundreds of strangers who knew nothing about her. The thought of that scared her so much, she was practically shaking.

The buzzing sound of an egg timer filled the air, bringing Nola's mind back to the present. "Time to flip over," she announced, glad for the distraction.

"Again?" Marnie rolled her eyes and squirted a glob of Neutrogena SPF 15 sunblock in her hand. "Hey, don't forget to check on Pip and Squeak."

"Thanks for reminding me." Nola would rather forget her little brothers even existed, but that wasn't an option. While her parents were at work for the day, the boys were her responsibility. She hated being the oldest, especially because it meant trying to keep King of the Antagonizers (Dennis) and The Mindless Follower (Dylan) in line. Marnie was so lucky — her older sister and only sibling, Erin, had left for college a week ago.

Nola leaned toward the end table, picked up her Motorola two-way radio, and clicked the ON button. "This is Nola, come in Dennis and Dylan." She waited for a few seconds before she repeated herself. "Come in Dennis and Dylan, or else Marnie is going to hunt you down!" Nola looked over at Marnie. "They're scared of you."

Marnie chuckled as she adjusted the top of her lime-green bandeau bikini. "I don't doubt that."

Nola had always been a shy, timid girl who usually went unnoticed in a crowd, despite her striking features (deep brown eyes, full, pouty lips, and tiny waist). She wasn't the type to raise her voice or get in someone's face, which is why her nine-year-old brothers ran around like the Rugrats. The only way to keep track of them was with two-way radios.

Suddenly Nola heard Dennis screaming through the crackling static, "We're on our way home, fathead!"

Nola's cheeks flushed. "Yeah, well . . . you're a . . ."

Marnie laughed out loud. "Good one, Nol."

"Shut up," Nola said, embarrassed. Comebacks were definitely not her specialty.

For some reason, Marnie leaped up from her seat and started doing jumping jacks. Nola watched her friend's petite, graceful feet with envy and then glanced down at her own. Over the summer, her feet had *grown*. A couple of weeks ago she had to order size 8½ Skechers from zappos.com and she'd been depressed ever since. She was really missing all her cute size 7 shoes.

"I can't sit still anymore," Marnie said through short

breaths. "Next Saturday is my birthday, *and* we're starting high school tomorrow. Freshman year, baby! Aren't you excited?"

Nola's heart began beating double-time. This was the conversation she'd been *dreading*. Although they'd talked about their freshman year at Poughkeepsie Central over the summer, fall had seemed so far away then. But now it was a reality: Her life would be drastically different — maybe even unrecognizable — tomorrow and there was nothing Nola could do about it. She hated feeling so frightened.

"I guess," Nola mumbled.

Marnie stopped jumping and crossed her arms in front of her chest. "You guess?"

Nola was only able to nod her head.

Marnie plopped down next to her. "You're flipping out, aren't you?"

"Kind of." Nola couldn't stop her lower lip from trembling.

"Remember our first day of kindergarten?" Marnie asked.

As if Nola could forget it. She closed her eyes for a second and every detail of that day came back to her. She thought about how she'd sat by herself at a long rectangular table, her legs dangling off the chair and her feet barely touching the olive-green carpet beneath her. She thought about how her mom had cuffed her tan pants so she wouldn't trip on the hems, and put her hair in a high ponytail so she would stop chewing on strands of it.

She could practically smell the Play-Doh and Clorox Wipes. She could see the cheerful banners that hung on the walls, and the coloring books scattered across the floor. But what stood out the most in Nola's mind was the sound of all the kids laughing and playing together before the bell rang, as well as the sound of her own crying when her mom left her behind for the very first time.

Nola smiled as she recalled the moment Marnie walked through the doors of the classroom several minutes later. She was wearing a pink polka-dot dress with puffy sleeves, white knee socks, and white patent-leather shoes with big, shiny buckles. She'd had a bow in her hair, too. Marnie definitely stood out, considering that most of the other kids were dressed for finger painting and freeze tag, not a *Showbiz Moms and Dads*–style beauty pageant. Nola was almost scared when Marnie flounced over to her table. Without even a "hello," Marnie had greeted a sniffling Nola with an affectionate pat on the head and a sweet grin.

Nola opened her eyes and saw that same grin on Marnie's face now.

"What was the first thing I said to you?" Marnie prompted.

"You promised to adopt me if my mom didn't come back," Nola replied.

"*And?*" Marnie urged.

"*And* you said, 'Let's play Barbies! We'll have the best time ever!'"

Marnie squeezed Nola's arm. "And we did! We had the best, Barbiest time *ever!*"

Nola simply loved Marnie at moments like these. She was an eternal optimist. The girl made lists of *everything*, and when a situation called for listing Pros and Cons, Marnie only listed the Pros. Which was exactly why Nola needed her.

"You'll do just fine tomorrow, Nol," Marnie said reassuringly.

Nola took a deep breath and exhaled. "I hope so."

"Besides, this is the year when everyone is going to notice us. We're *way* cuter now. I mean, we could totally shoot for the top five guys on my Crush List. Maybe I could even go for number *one*."

Nola leaned over and picked up Marnie's glass. Then she peered into it carefully.

"What are you doing?" Marnie asked.

"Just checking to see if someone spiked your lemonade." Nola grinned.

Marnie swatted her on the arm. "I can't help it. Think of all the great people we're going to meet and all the parties we'll get invited to and all the boys that we're going to kiss. Dah! I'm going to give myself a heart attack."

The girls laughed in unison.

"You're delirious from the heat, Marn," Nola said. "Don't you realize that we're *freshmen*? We're the bottom feeders on the food chain. Maybe even lower."

"Leave that to me," Marnie said slyly. "In a few weeks, we'll be two of the most popular girls in our class. *Everyone* will know us and adore us. And of course, no matter what happens, we'll always have each other. Promise."

Nola gave her friend a sideways glance. She wasn't sure she liked the way that sounded. She had been fine with flying under the radar in middle school. Why mess with that now? However, when she looked into Marnie's bright blue eyes, she saw that they were sparkling with excitement.

Maybe I shouldn't worry so much, Nola thought. Marnie had never broken a promise in her life. So Nola breathed a deep sigh of relief.

"Okay, *now* I'm psyched!" Nola exclaimed, raising her own tumbler of lemonade. "To ninth grade!"

Marnie clinked the rim of her glass against Nola's. "No, to the most spectacular year of our lives!"

Nola smiled widely. She liked the sound of that much better.

Chapter 2

THINGS TO DO THE MORNING BEFORE
MY FIRST DAY OF HIGH SCHOOL

1) Go for a run. Take the long route and try for ten-minute miles. (And don't forget to wear the sports bra this time!)
2) Use extra-conditioning hot oil treatment in the shower.
3) Clean out tote bag.
4) Find missing silver hoop earrings.
5) Create KILLAH OUTFIT!
6) Remind Nola to bring an extra five-subject notebook.
7) CALL ERIN BACK!!!

Thanks to her overactive, list-happy brain, Marnie Fitzpatrick didn't get much sleep after she left Nola's place late Monday night. So at 6 A.M. the following morning, Marnie was not enthusiastic about going on her run.

She stumbled out of the house, wiping at her eyes and yawning uncontrollably. She stretched on the front porch for a while as the sun continued to rise through the clouds. She could feel the cool, crisp wind through her mesh running shorts, but even that didn't energize her. Soon Marnie realized that there was only one solution: Make a pit stop at the Dunkin' Donuts on Main Street and buy a twelve-ounce cup of Turbo Iced Coffee.

Ten minutes later, she was outside the store, vigorously stirring her drink with a large straw. She finished it in about twelve big gulps and then strode down her favorite jogging route through the southwest corner of Poughkeepsie, where all the nice houses with landscaped yards and BMWs in the driveways were located.

Nola's beautiful, mauve Victorian house was nestled there, on quaint, peaceful Willow Bend, while Marnie and her family lived a few blocks away, right on the corner of Generic and Suburbia. In Marnie's neighborhood, the houses were smaller, the cars were less flashy, and the people were friendlier. Still, she preferred hanging out at Nola's house and jogging through her area — Marnie couldn't help it that she liked nice things.

And, nice things were harder to come by at the Fitzpatrick residence as of late, especially since Marnie's parents had separated, and her dad had moved to

Connecticut. Marnie didn't like thinking about that, but it was difficult not to when she ran. Her brain was just as much a part of the exercise as her legs were.

The caffeine really kicked in thirty minutes later, when Marnie returned to her modest three-bedroom yellow ranch house on St. Anne's Road. She dashed inside and showered, exfoliated, hot-oiled, and styled her naturally wavy blonde hair in record-breaking time. She emptied out her tote bag onto the floor and reorganized the contents. She found her silver hoop earrings in the pocket of her old tattered Levi's. She texted Nola — XTRA NTBK PLS! — and left a message on her older sister Erin's voice mail. But the most daunting task was left unfinished — she had to pick out what to wear on her first day of high school.

This decision could make or break her reputation — she knew that all too well. Four years ago, Marnie had sat at Erin's feet and watched her dive into her closet in search of the foolproof, I-dare-you-to-stop-staring-at-me-because-I'm-just-that-perfect outfit. And it had worked. Erin became the "it girl" of Poughkeepsie Central's student body the minute she set a stacked-heel Mary Jane onto the school grounds.

The past four years had been known as "The Erin Era." Right before graduation, Erin had been crowned queen of the senior prom and had even ridden on a float in the local firemen's parade. As for Marnie, she was well liked growing up, but she never came close to Erin's you-must-bow-down-before-me status. But lately Marnie had been telling herself, *This year all that could change.*

After weeks of putting together sample ensembles, Marnie had narrowed it down to two: a short, dark indigo denim skirt from Abercrombie paired with a crisp white button-down, a tiny yellow vintage knit vest, and gold Steve Madden ballet flats; *or* a tight-fitting green V-neck sweater, Lucky Brand white, cropped jeans with a multicolored, striped silk tie belt, *and* her pink canvas Keds slip-ons. All of the clothes were from last season and bought on clearance, but as always, Marnie focused on the positive. Both choices sent a similar message — *Marnie Fitzpatrick is totally cute* — but only one would make the statement with an exclamation point.

At precisely 7:15 A.M., Nola was in Marnie's room, clutching a Mead five-subject notebook and gazing at Options 1 and 2, which were lying on top of Marnie's neatly made sleigh bed.

"So tell me what you think already! We're losing precious time!" Marnie's blood was pumping with so much adrenaline and iced coffee that she was about to combust.

Nola shrugged her shoulders. "I don't know. Do you have anything else?"

Marnie, clad in boxers and a tank, stopped rifling through her glittery pink makeup bag long enough to throw Nola a death stare. "Um . . . NO!"

Nola let out a hearty laugh. "I'm kidding."

"Not funny," Marnie growled, and then returned her attention to her bag of tricks. She found the caramel-colored lip gloss Erin had given her before she left for Penn State and held it up like she'd won a trophy.

Nola brought the denim skirt to her waist and posed in front of Marnie's mirror. "Don't you think this is too short, Marn?"

"Yeah, that's the point." Marnie peered down at her lower half and smiled. Her legs did look a lot better now that her skin had some more color.

Nola shuffled over to the corner of Marnie's room, set the notebook down on Marnie's desk, and picked up the old tattered Levi's that were hanging over her white swivel chair. "What about these? They look super comfy."

"*Comfy?*" Marnie gave Nola a quizzical look. "Do you think the Mighty Erin Fitzpatrick would be caught dead in anything *comfy*? Do you think Sawyer Lee or Jason Naperella or Chris Gates would want to date *comfy*?"

"Ew, why would you want to impress *those* guys?" Nola sat on the swivel chair and spun around a few times.

Marnie shook her head. When it came to boys, Nola was *so* clueless. Sawyer, Jason, and Chris were numbers one, two, and three on her Crush List! How could she *not* want to impress them? Especially Sawyer. He had been the object of Marnie's devout adoration since she saw him skating on the half-pipe at Waryas Park in fourth grade. He had olive-colored skin, black spiky hair that was gelled to the max, and these amazing dark eyes. Marnie practically had a conniption every time he crossed her path.

"And I wish you'd stop obsessing about Erin," Nola added.

"Easy for you to say." Marnie stepped in front of the mirror and frowned. "Erin has always gotten to be *her* first, so I'm just stuck with the label of 'Erin's little sister' for all eternity."

Suddenly Marnie's phone began vibrating on her dresser. She scrambled for it and then sighed when she saw who it was.

"Hello?"

Erin's voice was barely audible.

"Hel-*lo*?" Marnie repeated loudly.

"*Shhhhhh*. My head is *killing* me," Erin groaned.

Marnie snickered. "Too much partying, I assume."

"Yeah, well, they call this place Happy Valley for a reason."

"What are you doing up so early?" Marnie asked.

"Ugh, I have this *stupid* eight A.M. required class. I mean, who can even *think* at this hour?" Erin mumbled.

"But you've been going to school at eight A.M. for twelve years now."

"Okay, *Mom*."

Marnie rolled her eyes. "So I called you back 'ASAP,' just like you asked me to. What's up?"

Erin sniffled. "Oh, right. I wanted to give you some sisterly advice for your first day at Po-Cen."

"Uh-huh." Marnie braced herself. Erin was known for her ultra-pretty face and hot clothes, *not* her warm and fuzzy personality.

"All you need to do is mention *me* as much as possible."

Marnie was utterly speechless.

"Seriously. Everyone *loved* me, so I suppose there's some hope for you because we, like, share the same DNA or whatever," she said coolly. "Oh and *don't* take any leftovers from my closet because then you'll just look like a poseur."

"Thanks, Erin. I've gotta go."

Erin coughed up a "peace out" before hanging up.

Nola nudged Marnie with the tip of her Skechers. "Just ignore her, Marn."

"I'll try," Marnie said wistfully.

Nola got up and put an arm around her. "Look at it this way. If Erin saw what *I* was wearing, she'd banish me to the far reaches of Wal-Mart."

Marnie smiled. If Nola only knew how gorgeous she looked in her baby-blue Lacoste polo shirt and a pair of long-frayed twill pants from Hollister. To top it all off, Nola had added the perfect accessory: one of her trademark homemade necklaces. Marnie stepped forward to get a closer look.

"Whoa, is this made out of *real* paper clips?" Marnie ran her finger along the lightweight chain of rainbow-colored plastic.

"Yes. I was in a nervous panic last night and I ran out of real materials, so I raided Dad's office supplies." Nola's signature crooked smile slowly revealed itself. "It's lame, right?"

"No, it's fabulous," Marnie said simply as she popped the collar on Nola's polo shirt.

And it was true. Nola may have been shy and quirky, but she had talent, creativity, and natural beauty that Marnie secretly envied. She had spent so much of her life being Nola's best friend, and at the same time living in Erin's shadow, that she hadn't really figured out what made *her* stand out. Yet here she was, less than an hour away from stepping into this new frontier, with the opportunity to totally reinvent herself.

Marnie wandered over to her bed and looked at Option 1 and Option 2 carefully. But at 7:46 A.M., when she walked to the bus stop arm in arm with Nola, she was wearing Option 3, which hopefully made this statement loud and clear:

Erin who?

Chapter 3

Nola took a deep breath as she stepped off the bus with Marnie and walked up the pathway leading toward Poughkeepsie Central. The enormous redbrick building looked very imposing. It sat on top of a steep hill, behind neatly trimmed shrubbery. On the main lawn, there was a statue of the prominent leader of the Native American tribe who gave the town its name, and the quote IMAGINE WHAT YOU'LL LEARN TOMORROW was engraved at his perfectly proportioned feet.

But by the time she reached homeroom 105 Nola couldn't even bring herself to imagine what tomorrow would have in store for her, especially because within her first fifteen minutes of high school, she suffered two brief, but very embarrassing moments:

First she'd tripped over a crack in the pathway and almost fell on top of a hottie. She just got a split-second, I'm-about-to-squash-you look at him, but she could see that he was tall, lean, and dressed in a pale yellow oxford shirt with the sleeves rolled up. Luckily, Marnie grabbed Nola by her backpack and saved her from knocking him down.

Then after that mini-fiasco, Nola started to hyperventilate, so she ran into the bathroom. The *boys'* bathroom, that is. Marnie came to the rescue again and yanked Nola out of there.

Nola was beyond flustered as she raced over to the bulletin board by the door, lugging her huge global studies textbook with her — when the bell had rung, she hadn't found a spot for it yet in her locker. Nola saw her name on the seating chart and tried to sprint to her desk. But as she worked her way through the crowd of students, she stepped on someone's toe. Really, *really* hard.

And where was Marnie Fitzpatrick? Down the hall in homeroom 104 with all the other A's through G's: i.e., nowhere near Nola.

The shriek was loud and high, as if it'd come from a parakeet who'd been caught in the mouth of a pit bull. But it was a girl who'd made that noise. A stunning blonde girl who appeared to have gotten dressed with her eyes closed this morning, but somehow had managed to look utterly fabulous. Nola knew from listening to Marnie-the-Fashion-Guru that you weren't supposed to cinch a bright orange floral housedress with a huge white belt or pair it with pointy red ankle boots (unless you were a celebrity or homeless or something), yet this girl was able to pull it off — no problem.

"I need to sit down," the girl moaned. A couple of people gathered around her and guided her to a desk.

The girl took off her ankle boot and began rubbing her foot.

Nola was practically in tears. "I'm sorry, I'm so, *so*, sorry." She must have said it more than once because the girl suddenly held up her hand and said, "What*ever!*" in an extremely annoyed voice.

"Do you want me to take you to the nurse?" Nola asked, even though she had no idea where the nurse's office was. Her heart was racing so fast she thought she might faint, and then they'd *both* have to be taken away in an ambulance.

"Maybe later, when I have some *feeling back in my toes!*" the girl snapped.

Nola just nodded and shrank toward the back of the room. She scrunched down in her seat and hid behind her global studies textbook. She was seconds away from breaking out in hives and she didn't want anyone to witness the horror. Marnie had seen it happen many times before and was quite handy with calamine lotion. Nola closed her watery eyes and wished really hard that somehow her best friend would appear and make everything okay.

Then there was a *tap-tap* on the other side of her textbook. She ignored it.

Tap-tap.

Nola began reading from some random chapter

in the middle of *Introduction to Global Studies:* "The main exports of Myanmar are timber and agricultural products."

Tap-tap.

The main exports of Myanmar are timber and agricultural products.

TAP-TAP.

THE MAIN EXPORTS OF MYANMAR ARE TIMBER AND AGRICULTURAL PRODUCTS!

TAP-TAP-TAP!

Nola reluctantly lowered her textbook. "What?" she asked briskly. Then she noticed that she was staring directly into the hazel eyes of a boy with an oval-shaped face and messy, light brown hair. She immediately looked away.

"Just wanted to see if you were still alive," he replied with a wink.

The last thing Nola needed right now was to go head to head with this annoying boy. Besides, she didn't have the guts to do it anyway. She raised *Introduction to Global Studies* in front of her face once again.

TAP-TAP.

Nola sighed in frustration and put the book down. "Yes?"

The boy grinned. "She's still alive, too."

Nola glanced over at the girl whose toe she nearly broke and saw the guy was right — she was happily chatting with a bunch of girls as if nothing had happened.

Finally there was a reason to smile. "Thanks," Nola said, grinning back.

"No problem." The boy spun around in his seat so that he was fully facing her. "But I wouldn't rule out a lawsuit."

Nola laughed in spite of her pre-hiveishness.

He extended his hand. "I'm Matt Heatherly."

Nola blinked a few times. She was a horrible conversationalist. It was one of the many drawbacks of being shy. "Oh . . . I'm Nola . . . Nola James," she stammered while shaking his hand, ever-so-lightly.

"Nice to meet you," Matt said. Then he wiped his hand on the bottom of his plain, charcoal-gray T-shirt.

Nola's paranoia immediately shifted into overdrive. *Whoa, what was that about? Are my palms really sweaty? Is there a wart on my finger? Or a booger?!*

But Matt acted like nothing was wrong. "So, which middle school did you go to? You don't look familiar."

Nola was still obsessing about that suspicious hand-wipe, so she could barely remember anything. "Um . . . you know," was all she could get out.

I'm destined to be a social leper!

Matt looked puzzled. "Huh. Well, I went to Arlington. It was okay, for a school built on a turnpike."

Nola couldn't believe it. Even though she was totally stressed out, she started laughing again.

"Our homeroom teacher is late," Matt said, gesturing at the clock above the chalkboard. "That's a good omen. Maybe school will be canceled forever and we'll be released into the wild."

"I wouldn't count on it." Nola scowled.

"You're right." Matt's grimace reappeared. "They'd probably just let us die in here."

Suddenly the classroom door flew open and a frantic woman with a rip in her dark beige stockings dashed in. She was completely disheveled and hiccuping. Nola breathed a sigh or relief: Someone was having a worse day than she was.

"I know, I know!" Loud hiccup. "I'm late!" The woman slammed her oversized, weather-beaten black satchel onto the top of her desk. "Get (hiccup) used to it."

Matt mouthed the words, "Oh boy" to Nola and turned back around in his seat very slowly. Nola swallowed hard. She didn't have to be a psychic to foresee that this teacher was going to be nothing but trouble.

"My name is Miss Lucas," the woman said as she rummaged through her bag and pulled out a folder stuffed with pieces of paper. After she'd rifled through it with great eagerness, she slammed it down on the desk as well. "We're skipping roll call today, people." Big scowl. "Can't (hiccup) find those stupid attendance sheets (hiccup) *anywhere!*"

Nola glanced at the clock. It was only 8:15 A.M. There was a whole day ahead of her and so far everything had gone wrong. But at least she'd met a nice boy.

That was always a good thing, wasn't it?

Chapter 4

The freshmen orientation assembly was held in the school's auditorium ten minutes later. A brightly colored sign proclaiming WELCOME FRESHMEN! was perched on an easel to the right of the stage. Marnie was sitting with the rest of her homeroom. Her right knee was bouncing up and down like a jackhammer as her eyes scanned the crowd for two things: cute guys and Nola.

When she spotted a few yummy morsels peppered throughout the crowd, Marnie's pulse picked up even more, but she nearly passed out when she saw Sawyer Lee. He was absolutely numero uno when it came to slacker hotness, and was looking mighty fine in a PacSun Hawaiian shirt and baggy jeans. The bright blond highlights he'd added to his spiked black hair made him look even edgier.

She thought about swinging by his locker later and getting her game on, but she'd thought about that a thousand times before and had done nothing. Even though he seemed so laid-back, Sawyer was just too cool to approach, and she was always tongue-tied around him. However, Marnie still couldn't deny the feeling that this year would be different. She just had to be patient. It was only the first day of school, after all.

Marnie glanced around and saw a few other fresh-faced hotties here and there, and when she saw Nola across the room talking to a cute boy of her own, Marnie could barely contain her glee. Then Nola looked up, caught a glimpse of Marnie, and gave her a limp wave along with her one-of-a-kind, "Don't mind me, I was born miserable" frowns. Marnie rolled her eyes. She was not going to let her best friend's sour mood affect her excitement.

Marnie felt a nudge from her left side. She turned and saw Sally Applebaum, who Marnie knew from middle school. Sally had curly hair that she tried to tame with barrettes and was so tiny that she was repeatedly turned away from the "big-kid" rides at amusement parks. Her dad worked as a clerk in the Dutchess County Comptroller's Office, but she acted as though he belonged to the UN and therefore deserved special diplomatic privileges. Despite that attitude, Sally was actually kind of nice. She was smart and well connected with the upperclassmen because her older sister, Judith, was a sophomore. Marnie was thankful to see a familiar face.

"Your outfit totally rocks," Sally said, trying not to let her voice rise above the principal's.

Marnie smiled. It was the fourth compliment she'd gotten on her Option 3 ensemble, which consisted of a camouflage cargo skirt, sky-high peep-toes from Kenneth Cole, and an Urban Outfitters black tee that had little silver peace signs scattered all over it. Nola had described the look as "very shock and awe."

"Thanks," she whispered back.

"When do you have lunch?" Sally asked.

Marnie reached into her pocket, pulled out the schedule she'd gotten in homeroom, and unfolded it. "Seventh period."

Sally let out a tiny squeal. "Yay! So do I. Want to sit together?"

Marnie looked up at Nola and saw her staring intently at the stage. She wondered whether or not Nola would mind if Sally joined them — whenever someone else was around Nola tended to get nervous and clam up. Marnie had hoped Nola would have grown out of that weirdness by now, but she hadn't.

This is Sally, though. Nola already knows her, Marnie thought. Still, she figured she might as well check with Nola first and see if it would make her uncomfortable.

"Hold on a sec," Marnie said as she pulled out her pink Razr phone. She typed a quick message and sent it off to Nola:

OK IF SALLY A. EATS W/ US?

Marnie glanced over at Nola again. She was frantically typing a message back. Within a few moments, Marnie's cell was vibrating in her hands.

SURE. WHO CARES?

Marnie's heart did a little flip. Maybe Nola was starting to mellow out.

Her phone shook again. Another message from Nola.

HOTTIE @ THE PODIUM!

When Marnie turned her attention to the stage, mellowness was the last thing on her mind.

Standing before Marnie and the entire freshman class was the tall, lean boy that Nola had almost trampled this morning. (Marnie had almost died of shame.) He was obviously a prep: Why else would he tuck his button-down shirt into a pair of khaki pants and wear dark brown slide-on loafers that perfectly matched his leather belt? He was delicious, too: short glossy brown hair, slightly flushed cheeks, large hands (he was an animated speaker), and a deep, yet cheerful voice. In a nutshell, he could be Ryan Gosling's long-lost brother.

Marnie leaned over to Sally. "Who *is* that?" She had to know, and she had to know N-O-W.

"Dane Harris," Sally said. "He was the vice president of the freshman class last year."

Marnie adjusted her skirt. "Does Judith know him?"

"Yeah, she says he's super-popular and sweet, but he hangs out with all the Majors — you know, the popular kids," Sally explained. "If you get into that inner circle, you're, like, golden."

Marnie turned her gaze back to Dane.

"I know how it is to feel as if you don't know what's going on around you," he was saying kindly. "So feel free to stop me in the hall and ask a question. I'll be more than happy to help. And if you're interested in joining student government, please come to lecture hall four next Thursday after school."

Marnie shivered with anticipation. She knew exactly where she would be next Thursday after dismissal, and who she'd be stopping in the hall later today. She just had to figure out what her question would be.

Dane finished his speech and the principal instructed the freshmen to go to their first class. As everyone made their way out of the auditorium, Marnie edged her way through the crowd until she reached Nola.

"Hey you," she said, pulling Nola in for a one-arm hug.

Nola grinned. "Why do I have the feeling that you'll be staying late after school in the near future?"

"Because you know me better than anyone else, that's why." Marnie giggled. "Are you holding up okay?"

Nola's smile vanished. "We don't have enough time to cover how horrible homeroom went without you."

"It's going to get better, Nol, I just know it."

"Yeah, we'll see," Nola replied unenthusiastically.

"Quick, let me take a look at your schedule," Marnie said as they walked toward their lockers, which were no more than a few feet away from each other. Nola handed over her schedule, and Marnie scanned it rapidly.

"Ugh," Marnie sighed in defeat.

Nola's brown eyes darkened with worry. "What's wrong?"

Marnie sighed. "You've got lunch sixth period, and I've got it seventh."

"Are you kidding?" Nola looked stricken.

"No, I'm not." Marnie was surprised, too. She'd never had lunch without Nola — it was the only time during the day when they could gossip and skim *In Touch* without interruption. As she read the rest of Nola's schedule, Marnie's shoulders slouched. "In fact, we don't have *any* classes together."

"This is not good, Marn," Nola said, her skin blanching.

Marnie immediately went into emergency mode. She wasn't about to let this mini-crisis get in the way of any awesomeness that was yet to come. "Don't worry, okay?

Maybe I can, like, switch my schedule around. I'll check with one of the guidance counselors." But before Marnie could provide Nola with any more comfort, the bell rang. Marnie grabbed her books from her locker, handed Nola her schedule, and gave her friend a full-on hug this time.

"Everything's going to work out," she said. "Promise."

And with that, Marnie sprinted off to her next class, believing every word she'd said.

Chapter 5

Lunchtime used to be a no-brainer for Nola. Every day from kindergarten until eighth grade, she and Marnie would sit and eat together, although Nola never really enjoyed the cuisine in the brown paper bag she'd brought from home. Nola's mom, Carol, was a doctor who had done some research and discovered that the school cafeterias in the region hadn't been providing their students with enough "healthy choices." Thus, since the age of five, Nola had gotten stuck with a variety of salads, or "lawn clippings," as Marnie had referred to them last year.

Back in grade school, when Nola had opened up Marnie's Powerpuff Girls lunch box, all she'd find was junk food with fun, neon-colored packaging that had phrases like BURSTING WITH FLAVOR! written on it. Nola was jealous, and rightfully so. Thankfully, Marnie began sneaking Nola some Milky Ways and extra bags of Doritos, never forgetting to give Nola a stick of cinnamon Trident so that Dr. James wouldn't smell the Polysorbate 80 on Nola's breath — the woman's nostrils were *that* strong.

In middle school, the girls would be off in their own little world during lunch, recapping what had happened in each class as if they hadn't spent all morning together. Those forty-two minutes had become precious to Nola; for once, she was able to relax and not worry about being called on by a teacher, or going up to the chalkboard to solve a math problem.

Yet all of that was in the past. Now Nola was holding a tray stacked with unhealthy items that her mother would never approve of, wondering what to do with herself. While the cafeteria wasn't too big, the scariest thing about it was the shape of the blue tables. They were *circular*, which meant that everyone seated around them could be included in a conversation, or a castle-defense-strategy plan like the Knights of the Round Table.

Nola glanced around and did a quick scan of the cafeteria. She did recognize a bunch of people from her old middle school: artsy Annika Holbrook, clownish David Presley, and brainiac Morgan Attenberg. But Nola didn't feel comfortable sitting down with any of them. She heaved a sigh of frustration and pictured Marnie in this exact situation. She could see her best friend sliding in next to Annika and complimenting her notebook doodles with the greatest of ease.

If only I could just get over myself, Nola thought.

"Hey Nola, over here," a voice called out.

Nola turned to the right and saw Matt Heatherly

waving her over to his table. He was sitting with two friends, a boy and a girl, who were flipping through a magazine. Nola grinned. Last year, she and Marnie had read *In Touch* during study hall and mocked silly headlines like LINDSAY AND PARIS'S SMACK-DOWN CATFIGHT! and NICOLE'S SECRET BOTOX CONFESSION! The familiar memory made her feel a little less anxious.

"Wanna sit down?" Matt asked.

Nola nodded, and he scooted over so that she could squeeze in next to him. "Thanks," she said.

Matt took the iPod buds out of his ears and began the introductions. "Nola, the Whacker across from you is Evan Sanders."

What is a Whacker? Nola gave Evan a quick once-over and tried to figure it out for herself. He had a Caesar-style haircut and was wearing a T-shirt that had COW TIPPING ANONYMOUS written on it.

Evan scratched his head and said, "Hey."

She was still stumped.

Matt pointed at the almond-eyed, black-haired girl next to Evan. "And this is Iris Santos."

"Token Filipino and resident Leek, thank you very much," she said with a funny little head bob.

Nola squinted in confusion.

"Oh, I'm sorry, I thought you'd learned the lingo already," Matt said.

Nola hadn't spoken to anyone other than Marnie since the assembly, so learning any type of lingo was pretty much out of the question.

Iris tossed her head again so that she could get her longish bangs out of her eyes. "I wouldn't bother. The whole thing is asinine."

Matt grabbed the magazine away from Evan and Iris. "Is it any more asinine than debating which brand of laptop provides the longest battery life?"

Nola saw that the magazine in question was *PC World* — a far, far cry from *In Touch*.

Evan tried repeatedly to get the magazine from Matt but was unsuccessful. "There's no debate on that. It's the HP ZT1190." He crossed his arms over his chest and said to Iris, "Don't you agree?"

"Totally," Iris replied confidently. "It's ideal for travel. I'll need something like that for all my debate team away-meets."

"And there you have it!" Matt declared proudly.

Nola stuffed her sloppy joe into her mouth and began chewing. There was no way she could keep up with these guys.

"Whatever, Matt. It's not like you don't fit under one of these dumb labels," Iris countered.

"Oh, I know I do," he said.

"Yeah, right," Evan said, finally snatching the magazine back from Matt.

Nola giggled.

"Evan, do something useful and pass my PowerBook this way," Matt said.

Evan slid the laptop across the table. Nola watched as Matt opened it up and maximized a window so a message board could appear.

"Some upperclassmen posted this dumb list on the school's intranet this morning so that us low-life frosh would know where we stand," Matt explained.

Nola scanned the list.

The Majors = the most popular kids
The Minors = wannabes
Whacker = computer nerd
Leek = leadership geek

And it went on and on.

"Wow," was the only thing Nola could say.

Evan checked his watch. "I gotta run to my locker. Keep an eye on my stuff, will ya?"

"You got it," Matt said.

"Wait, I'll go with you," said Iris. "I forgot my Moto Q." But before she walked away with Evan, she turned to Nola and said, "Sweet necklace, by the way. Did you make that?"

"Yes," Nola said bashfully. "Thanks a lot."

And then there were two.

Nola's heart rate shot up to red-alert levels. She had no idea what to do, so she concentrated on eating her French fries. Meanwhile Matt plugged his iPod into his PowerBook and began downloading a bunch of songs off of iTunes. Nola peeked at the band names: Gnarls Barkley, Panic! at the Disco, White Stripes, BT, Pete Yorn. It was beginning to seem as though a hard-core music freak lurked inside the not-too-shabby-looking body of this charming, funny boy.

She also noticed that Matt was wearing a blue rubber wristband that had RF FOREVER stamped on it — was RF a cool band she didn't know about, or something else, like a special girl in his life? Her curiosity was instantly piqued.

"So, I suppose you're a real TM, huh?" Matt asked suddenly.

Nola stared at him, baffled.

"A troublemaker," he clarified. "Not a school label, but . . ."

She giggled at the thought of someone characterizing her that way. "No, I'm afraid not."

"You sure?"

Nola chuckled again. "Positive."

Matt leaned over and picked a fry off of Nola's plate,

as if they'd known each other forever. "Could've fooled me. I thought the way you stepped on Lizette Levin's foot was the definition of Troublemaker."

At the mere mention of *that* name, Nola's windpipe completely closed up as if she was having an allergic reaction. Once Nola's eyes began watering, Matt became concerned.

"Are you okay?" he asked.

Nola swallowed hard. She was anything but okay.

Lizette Levin.

If Marnie only knew how badly she'd messed up. . . .

Chapter 6

Less than an hour later, Marnie was in the cafeteria, staring at the table occupied by the infamous Lizette Levin. Erin's best friend, Rachel, was Lizette's cousin, so over the summer Marnie had to endure countless stories about Lizette's country-club pedigree, her recent "holiday" in Sweden, and all the good-looking, well-bred Scandinavian boys she'd met. In fact, the way Rachel went on and on, it was as if the girl had super powers and could turn a pair of Old Navy jeans into a Prada dress with a snap of her French-manicured fingers.

Although she'd heard a lot about Lizette, up until now all Marnie had seen of her was one blurry picture on Rachel's Nokia flip phone. Lizette had attended Arlington Middle School, so Marnie and Nola hadn't had the pleasure of making her acquaintance yet. The only reason Marnie knew what Lizette looked like was because Sally elbowed her in the side during lunch and said, "Wait, Lizette Levin actually *eats*?" then pointed at a Mischa Barton–esque girl dressed in a funky blend of vintage clothes, who was licking a grape Popsicle.

Marnie couldn't have imagined the girl any differently. From what she'd heard, über-popular Lizette had grown up in Manhattan and was a daddy's girl who got whatever she wanted. In fact, Lizette's father was a bestselling mystery author, who had taken a writer-in-residence position at Vassar College once he split up with her mother. With one parent living in Sweden and the other on campus by day and in the study by night, Lizette was able to do as she pleased. And if that involved wearing clothes that looked as though they belonged on a mental patient, so be it.

Sally nudged Marnie again. "C'mon, let's go sit over there." Sally gestured to a table filled with girls from their middle school. Marnie gripped her tray tightly. Even though she would have been most comfortable sharing her lunch with Nola, Sally Applebaum and her group were probably the next best thing.

But when Marnie glanced over at Lizette and her pretty, stylish friends, she couldn't calm the voice inside her head, which kept saying, *What would Erin do?* Marnie knew the answer to that: cozy up to as many Majors as possible.

Besides, from this distance, Lizette seemed really nice. She was smiling and laughing and being playful with everyone around her. There was nothing to be afraid of.

Except for total humiliation, of course.

"Sally, there's room at that table," Marnie said while motioning to Lizette's section.

Sally looked at Marnie as if she'd suggested they run across the football field in their underwear. "You're joking, right?"

"No," she replied.

"Marnie," Sally said seriously. "If we go over there, we'll get dissed in front of everybody."

Marnie knew that the odds of that happening were high, but she still felt it was worth the risk. "Don't you want to meet new people?"

"You can go ahead if you want to," Sally said as she walked away.

Marnie didn't follow her. Instead, she slowly approached Lizette's table. With each step, Marnie felt a few hints of worry, but she tried blocking it out by focusing on her posture. She thought this relaxation technique was better than any meditation CD on the market.

When Marnie got within arm's reach of Lizette, she brought her shoulders back and stood up straight. She contracted her stomach muscles, too, and took a deep breath. Then she waited silently for a few seconds, trying to listen for an opening in the conversation. Lizette was telling a story at warp speed.

"And then this *freak* girl crushes my toe with her

giant elephant feet! And then I went to the nurse after homeroom, and she told me that if it weren't for these boots, one of my toes might have been amputated!"

It wasn't long before Lizette became aware of Marnie's presence and looked up at her with a confused expression on her face.

Just be friendly, Marnie thought. *And don't forget to breathe.*

"You want something?" Lizette asked.

Marnie's eyes darted around the table. The other girls were staring at her crossly, as if she'd interrupted a new episode of *My Super Sweet 16.*

"Yeah, I was wondering if I could sit with you guys," Marnie replied with a soft smile.

Lizette grinned, and the girl sitting next to her began whispering in her ear. Marnie couldn't hear what the girl was saying, but she did notice the girl had a slight gap in her front teeth, which was unusual-looking and kind of cool. The whispering went on for way longer than normal, though. Then Lizette started to giggle.

If this didn't stop soon, Marnie would have to contact the FBI and ask to join the "I'm a teenage girl who just got clowned" version of the Witness Protection Program.

Gap-toothed Girl was done whispering. She leaned over the table and said something to the redhead.

Marnie peered over her shoulder and saw that everyone at Sally's table was watching her.

This is a nightmare.

Marnie spun around and was about to bolt out the door, but before she could, Lizette looked up at her again and said, "I guess so. There's a spot by Grier."

"Thanks." Marnie smiled weakly. She had a feeling that when she had turned around for a second, they had planted something gross on her chair and were waiting for her to sit on it. She cautiously made her way over to the vacant seat next to the redhead with freckles all over her cheeks.

When Marnie sat down, she sighed in relief. Grier looked pretty harmless and things were looking up.

Gap-toothed Girl picked at her hamburger bun and sneered at Marnie as if she'd stolen her boyfriend. "So what's your name?"

She swallowed hard. "Marnie Fitzpatrick."

Lizette's eyes grew wide with recognition. "Wait, are you *Erin* Fitzpatrick's sister?"

Things were definitely looking up.

"Yeah, I am."

Lizette grinned. "Wow, how awesome is that? I can't wait to tell Rachel I finally met you."

Marnie was overjoyed with this response, until Lizette turned to Gap-toothed Girl and whispered again. More giggling. Then Gap-toothed Girl let out a full-blown cackle and said, "Oh, so *that's* who she is."

Marnie knew that this was her chance to save what was left of her dignity. She started thinking of ways to get out of this mess. For instance, she could fake a nasty leg cramp and say she needed to walk it off, or she could text Nola and ask her to run some sort of military-style diversion.

All of a sudden, there was a collective gasp at the table.

"Dane Harris," Grier muttered under her breath.

"He's coming this way," Gap-toothed Girl said, her voice high-pitched and squeaky.

It's a sign, Marnie thought. *I can't leave now.*

Her hands went numb when she saw Dane striding across the cafeteria. His green eyes were gleaming to match his bright smile and he was effortlessly tossing an orange from one hand to the other, the long muscles in his arms rippling. Maybe he was on the basketball team, too. The thought of seeing Dane in shorts and a jersey made Marnie's head spin.

But Lizette was the picture of calm. "Brynne, you'll break a blood vessel in your eye if you stare at him any harder."

Marnie and Grier both laughed at Lizette's wit, but

Gap-toothed Girl aka Brynne crossed her arms over her chest and pouted.

Grier pulled out some Stila lip gloss from her neon-yellow clutch. "Why do you think he's walking over here?"

Lizette gave her Popsicle another lick. "He's probably looking for a party."

"How do you know?" Brynne asked.

"I hung out with him a little at the Beekman Country Club this summer," Lizette said, seemingly unfazed by Dane's gorgeousness. "Parties were all he talked about. You gotta wonder how for real he is, though. I mean, I think he's wearing *Dockers*."

Parties, huh? Marnie's face lit up with excitement. She just happened to know about a very cool birthday party next Saturday, and in a few minutes, everyone else at Lizette Levin's table — including the ultra-hot Dane Harris — would know about it, too.

Thursday, Sept 6, 5:45 P.M.

marniebird: *hey lady! how come u weren't on the bus after school? i looked for u @ ur locker and u weren't there either*

nolaj1994: *sorry mom picked me up early. she got called into the hospital and my dad already left for his flight 2 san fran*

marniebird: *ah the drama*

nolaj1994: *it never ends*

marniebird: *stuck watching pip & squeak again?*

nolaj1994: *2 days in a row. i'm soooo lucky* ☹

marniebird: *that's 2 bad. mom's taking me to amici's 4 pizza. i wanted u 2 come so we could trade first day stories!!!*

nolaj1994: *ugh*

marniebird: *c'mon, i wanna hear. but quick cuz we're leaving in a few*

nolaj1994: *honestly i think i blocked it all out*

marniebird: *was it really that bad?*

nolaj1994: *when my mom picked me up, i begged her 2 homeschool me, or send me 2 apex tech. u get 2 keep the toolbox even if u don't graduate*

marniebird: *LOL. well what about that certain BOY i saw u talking 2 during assembly?*

nolaj1994: *u mean matt? he's just in my homeroom*

marniebird: *u 2 seemed pretty friendly. Tee-hee!*

nolaj1994: *did ur peep-toes cut off all the oxygen 2 ur brain?*

marniebird: *my my, defensive, aren't we?*

nolaj1994: *promise 2 tell u everything 2morrow when u sleep over. why don't u tell me about YOUR day?*

marniebird: *let's put it this way, it was !!!!!!!!!!!!!!!!!!!!!!!!!!!!!!!!!!*

nolaj1994: *that good, huh?*

marniebird: *yep. and my whole crush list is out of whack now that i know perfection like DANE exists*

nolaj1994: *hold on, let me find the drool emoticon. btw, he is the complete opposite of SL*

marniebird: *?*

nolaj1994: *clean-cut, all-american, belongs in a tommy hilfiger ad*

marniebird: *totally. i was soooo close 2 talking 2 DH @ lunch today, but everyone else was hogging him*

nolaj1994: *who did you sit with?*

marniebird: *LIZETTE LEVIN! can u believe it?*

nolaj1994: *actually she's in my homeroom*

marniebird: *that's right! i wonder why i didn't notice her in ur group @ assembly. her clothes really make her stand out.*

nolaj1994: *no idea*

marniebird: *wait, she mentioned something @ lunch about being at the nurse*

nolaj1994: *she did?*

marniebird: *yeah, she said some freak girl with giant elephant feet stepped on her toe*

nolaj1994: *FREAK GIRL?*

marniebird: *uh-huh. did u c what happened?*

nolaj1994: *GIANT ELEPHANT FEET? really, she said GIANT ELEPHANT FEET?*

marniebird: *whoa! it was U!*

nolaj1994: **gulp**

marniebird: *hahahahahahahahaha*

nolaj1994: *glad u think it's funny*

marniebird: *oh she's probably 4gotten all about it by now*

nolaj1994: *u think so?*

marniebird: *doubt it, i was just trying 2 b nice*

nolaj1994: *ha ha*

marniebird: *ugh, mom is calling me. don't worry about LL, and remember, full recaps tomorrow night, u promised*

nolaj1994: *i know, i know. have fun.*

marniebird: *i will.*

nolaj1994: *LYLAS*

marniebird: *LYLAS*

Chapter 7

Friday-night sleepovers at Nola's house had been a tradition since fourth grade. A couple hours before Marnie's arrival, Nola would blow up the AeroBed, put out the Peanut Lovers' Chex Mix, and decide whether the mood called for clay masks or pedicures. She also had to make sure the room was Dennis- and Dylan-proof — before she got a lock for her door, she had to shove her toy chest in front of it. But the most important part of the evening was the movie. Tonight was no exception.

Marnie tore open the Netflix package on Nola's desk and laughed. *"Big Momma's House 2?"*

Nola rubbed some gooey clay mask onto her cheeks. "I *really* hope it lives up to *Big Momma's House*."

"But sequels are always worse than the original." Marnie popped the disc into the DVD player, and then plopped down on the AeroBed next to Nola.

"Very true, especially in the case of *Deuce Bigalow: European Gigolo*." Nola handed the jar of clay mask to Marnie. "But isn't watching a horrible movie the whole point?"

Marnie rolled her eyes. "How many times do I have to say I'm sorry?"

Up until a few months ago, Friday night movies had

had only one theme — hot guys. The girls would rent whatever flick was starring the most gorgeous male celebrity of the moment. But then one night, Marnie insisted that they watch the Olsen twins' movie *New York Minute* because she'd been obsessed with Jared Padalecki (aka Dean from *Gilmore Girls*). It was by far the most terrible movie they'd ever seen, and since then Nola had decided that the theme would change from hot guys to the worst films of all time.

"Once more would be nice," Nola replied, smirking.

Marnie sighed. "Nola James, will you pretty please with Splenda on top forgive me for making you watch *New York Minute*?"

"I don't know. That's two hours of my life I'll never get back." Nola tried to smile again, but the mask was hardening.

"You really know how to hold a grudge," Marnie said as the opening credits rolled.

"It's a gift," Nola mumbled. The mask had stiffened so much, her lips were puckering.

Marnie reached into her overnight bag and pulled out a bag of Smartfood white cheddar-flavored popcorn. "I brought extra provisions for the movie. My mom loves this stuff."

Nola wrinkled her nose. "But we always have Chex Mix."

"Change will do you good, Nol." Marnie opened the bag and took a whiff. "Oh, yeah." She offered some to Nola.

"I'm sticking with the mix, thanks."

"Fine, more for me then." Marnie pulled her bare knees up to her chest and stretched her lavender cotton nightshirt over them. "So when are you going to tell me more about this Matt guy?"

Nola shrugged. *Typical boy-crazy Marnie.* In third grade, she had her first crush on the class troublemaker, Pete Carucci. Now Marnie's tally on her Crush List was in the double digits. She even had an ex-boyfriend who provided her with plenty of kissing experience.

As for Nola, her crush tally was in the single digits, she had one kiss (via Truth or Dare), and zero ex- *or* current boyfriends. Nola wasn't thrilled with these numbers, but she didn't see how she could improve them. Marnie could afford to have boys on the brain all the time because she was assertive and could talk to them with confidence. But Nola didn't have it as easy. When she liked a boy, she couldn't even breathe normally around him. It was a condition that Marnie called "boy-related asthma."

"I've told you everything. He's in my homeroom, I had lunch with him and his friends, and we traded personal info after our advanced, brainiacs-only freshman physics class. Voilà." Nola wasn't sure what more there was to say. Matt seemed interesting and he was definitely cute, but unlike Marnie, she didn't salivate over every guy.

"So who are these friends of his? Anyone cool?" Marnie asked.

Nola pretended she didn't hear Marnie and poked at her clay-covered skin. "How long do I have to leave this on?"

Marnie picked up the jar off Nola's bed and read the label. "Fifteen to twenty minutes."

Nola groaned. Her pores felt as though they were covered in cement. She should have given herself a pedicure instead.

"Well, I bet he knows Dane Harris," Marnie said with a mouth full of popcorn.

"You think so?"

"Whoa, you should have heard all the things Lizette said about Dane during lunch today," Marnie replied, returning her gaze to Big Momma.

If Nola's lips had been able to move, they would have turned into a frown. Marnie had lunch with Lizette *again*, even though she knew that Lizette thought Nola was a freak? Where was the loyalty?

"Like what?" Nola asked, only she didn't particularly care.

"Lizette told Grier — oh, I mean Grier Hopkins, the

redhead in Lizette's troop who hangs with Brynne Callaway — you know, the snotty brunette with the gap between her teeth? Anyway, Lizette said she heard from a few people in her lit class that Dane is a *mega* Major. Like, he runs with the seniors and goes to all their parties and he's supposedly friends with everyone. That's how cool he is."

"Well if he's a mega Major, what does that make us?" Nola asked. "Minor Minors?"

"Of course not!" Marnie said emphatically. "You and I are anything but wannabes."

"Yeah, well, we're nothing special either."

"Speak for yourself!" Marnie quipped.

Nola rolled her eyes. "What about the *Marnie-James?* You know, like Mary-Janes."

Marnie laughed. "That's terrible, Nol."

"I know. That's why I like it." Nola smiled.

Marnie sighed. "Can we get back to Dane now?"

"Sure. But I must admit I'm surprised that you haven't mentioned Sawyer all night." Nola was used to Marnie listing Sawyer's drool-inducing qualities on the eights of every hour à la the local forecasts on The Weather Channel.

"Sawyer will always be my red-hot skater fantasy, but what can I say? He has officially slipped to number two on the Crush List." Marnie threw a piece of popcorn in the air and caught it in her mouth. "Dane is number one now."

Nola was stunned. Sawyer had been Marnie's ultimate crush for five years, and he had only been kicked out of the number one spot once — when Marnie fell for Weston Briggs, her boyfriend in eighth grade. Nola had tried to warn Marnie about that guy, but she didn't listen and it caused her a lot of heartbreak, especially when Weston broke things off after almost four months and then moved away with his family. Nola knew it probably wasn't the best idea to caution Marnie, but she figured if she was subtle about it, it might be okay.

"It's nice that he's popular, but he could also be an idiot like Weston," Nola said matter-of-factly. A second later, she regretted her words. *Ugh, why don't I just take a vow of silence already?*

Marnie bristled a bit. "Not all guys are like Weston and not all popular people are idiots. Look at Lizette. She's really down-to-earth and outgoing."

Nola's stomach twisted into a knot. Was Marnie trying to make a point or something? "Yeah, well, I suppose. If you don't mind it when she calls your best friend a freak."

Marnie giggled. "With giant elephant feet!"

Nola could feel her face turning red. Luckily Marnie couldn't see it. But Nola felt so unnerved that she got up and went into her private bathroom to wash the mask off her skin, even though she hadn't left it on more than five minutes.

The cool water felt good on Nola's face. Once she rinsed it off, she patted her face dry with a towel. She still felt flushed, though, like she had yesterday in homeroom. Nola looked down at her feet. They *were* such monstrosities. She couldn't help but feel self-conscious about them. Usually Marnie was sensitive to things like this. But Nola couldn't help but notice that tonight she seemed a little different. Her teasing had an edge to it. Nola shook her head and told herself she was just imagining things.

When Nola came back into the bedroom, Marnie had paused the DVD and was running her fingers through the mane of her favorite stuffed animal — Billy the Lion.

"You don't have giant elephant feet," Marnie said simply. "And if I'd known you were the one who was being called Freak Girl, I would have told Lizette off. You know that, right?"

Nola grinned. "I do. Thanks."

The *ping* sound of Nola's IM got her attention. She

went over to her desktop computer and woke up its sleeping monitor with a tug of the mouse. She glanced at the IM window and saw a message.

mheatherly: *u busy? got a question for ya*

"Who is it?" Marnie asked.

Nola swallowed hard. She knew the instant she said it was Matt, Marnie was going to flip out and be totally annoying and obsessed and over-the-top.

"Um, it's someone from my physics class," she said.

"Uh-huh," Marnie said, smiling.

Nola knew she wasn't fooling anyone. "I'm just going to ignore it."

Marnie seemed to take this as an invitation to interfere. She jumped off the AeroBed, dashed to the desk, and looked at the screen over Nola's shoulder. "Wow, you are such a babe-magnet! He's gonna ask you out!"

Nola hip-checked Marnie. "He is not. This is probably about our homework assignment."

"That's just an excuse to talk to you outside of school." Marnie tried to put her hands near the keyboard, but Nola swatted them away. "Don't you know anything about guys?"

Nola sat down and typed back:

nolaj1994: *sure, what's up?*

"You amaze me, Nola. That was the most boring response ever," Marnie huffed.

"What was I supposed to say?"

Marnie looked puzzled. "I don't know. Anything's better than 'what's up.' Like 'fire away' or 'only if you gimme some sugah.'"

Nola raised her eyebrows. "Gimme some *sugah*?"

"What? That's supercute!"

"No, it's not!"

mheatherly: *wondering if u were doing anything on tues*

Nola gulped. Marnie was right! He *was* asking her out. This was utterly shocking. "What do I do now?" she asked nervously.

Marnie's blue eyes sparkled as she let out a joyful yelp. "This is so great! Okay, tell him you're busy. No! Wait! Tell him that maybe you're busy, or maybe you're not."

Nola could barely make out what Marnie was saying, she was talking so fast. In fact, Marnie seemed more excited about Matt than *Nola* was. "Hold on, why am I telling him that I'm busy? I don't have any plans."

"Because, silly, you want him to think you are *so* popular that you're booked until Thanksgiving, that's why!" Marnie cried, rolling her eyes.

nolaj1994: *nope*

"You're bad at this." Marnie retreated to the AeroBed in defeat.

Nola waited with anticipation for Matt's reply. What was he going to say next? She was surprised by how curious and energized she was.

mheatherly: *great*

A few seconds went by without another word. Nola's breathing suddenly became shallow and labored.

mheatherly: *i was looking ahead in the syllabus. we have a quiz in 2 wks. thought we could b study buddies*

"Oh boy," Nola exhaled.

Marnie heard her though, so she leaped up and ran to Nola's side. She read Matt's IM over Nola's shoulder. "Nol, that's . . . AWESOME!" she shouted into Nola's ear.

Nola shoved Marnie away. "What's the matter with you? He just said he wants to study."

"Yeah, right. He wants to date you!" Marnie did a little two-step that had Nola laughing in spite of herself.

nolaj1994: *cool. ttyl*
mheatherly: *c ya*

"Okay, let's get down to business," Nola said after she shut off her computer and flopped down on the AeroBed.

Marnie turned off the lights, un-paused the movie, and sat down next to Nola. "Yeah, well, tomorrow we have *real* business to attend to. Like, shopping for your date-with-Matt outfit!"

Nola grabbed Billy the Lion and bopped Marnie on the head. "Shhhh. Big Momma's talking."

For the next ninety minutes, the crunch of Chex Mix and popcorn was the only sound in Nola's room, with the exception of several belly laughs. It was the most comfortable Nola had felt since the day before yesterday, and she didn't want it to end. Mondays just always came too soon.

Chapter 8

BIRTHDAY OUTFIT ACCESSORIES MUST-HAVES
1) Delicate chandelier earrings from Anthropologie
2) Aldo platform wedges for maximum height
3) A chunky ring — maybe the turquoise from BCBG?
4) Patterned tights and/or leggings

On Saturday afternoon, Marnie and Nola walked arm in arm down Main Street in nearby Pleasant Valley to Past 'N Perfect, a chic little consignment shop that Marnie had been dying to go to. She loved hanging out in this area on the weekends. Poughkeepsie was an okay town to live in, but the only place to shop was the Galleria, and that got boring *real* fast. In Pleasant Valley, though, there were unique stores to browse in, tiny cafés that made delicious blended iced mochas, and specialty shops that sold gilt-trimmed stationery, beautiful flower arrangements, and homemade chocolates. It was a great spot to lose oneself in, especially on a crisp autumn day.

Marnie wrapped her gray cardigan around herself when the breeze picked up, blowing some red-and-orange leaves across the sidewalk. She stared at the store window, where a mannequin was dressed in the most unusual outfit. It might not be right for Nola's study date with Matt or for Marnie's birthday party — it was part boho, part punk, and very sassy. However, it was extremely eye-catching. Marnie adored bright colors and odd patterns, but she never quite knew how to work them. At least, not in the supercool way Lizette Levin did.

She felt a tap on her shoulder and turned around to see Nola, looking kind of tired. "Please tell me this is the last store," Nola groaned.

Marnie snickered. Nola would always be a shopping amateur. "I can't help it that you refuse to buy anything."

Nola rolled her eyes and pushed open the door. Marnie skipped in behind her. When she glanced around the shop, she couldn't stop smiling. There were racks and racks of vintage clothes, quirky-looking shoes, designer handbags, and shelves filled with all sorts of berets, caps, and cowboy hats.

Marnie wandered around, touching all the fabrics with her fingertips, wondering if she might find a killer dress somewhere in this dizzying maze of fashion. Her mom had just gotten a big commission check for the four-bedroom two-bath colonial she'd sold a few months ago, so she'd given Marnie some extra spending money this morning. It felt good to have some cash in her purple star-shaped change purse, but she wasn't sure she should use it. Her parents had just finalized their divorce, and Erin's college tuition was hanging over her mom's head. *But,* next week was her birthday. Marnie tried to tell herself that it was okay to be selfish sometimes, but it didn't stick. Thinking about everyone else was what she did best.

When Marnie looked up, she spotted Nola in a fuzzy arctic hunter's cap, sitting on one of the red couches that were most likely reserved for bored boyfriends. Marnie sighed. Did she always have to push Nola to do *everything*?

"What's with you?"

Nola tugged at her hood strings. "Nothing. It's just that . . . this place isn't really my style."

Marnie took a closer look at what Nola was wearing: a navy-blue hoodie, white T-shirt, and a pair of faded jeans. There couldn't be a more generic outfit in the universe. Marnie had a feeling that Nola, who was by far the best-looking girl in their class, wore this type of nondescript clothing so nobody would notice her.

But that was the opposite of what Marnie was going for these days.

"I'm sure if you look around, you'll find something

nice," Marnie said patiently as she pulled out a fuchsia halter dress with an asymmetrical hemline. "Whoa, isn't this *hawt*?"

Nola scrunched up her nose.

Marnie walked over to the full-length mirror and held the dress up in front of her. "You can't live in pants forever, Nol. It isn't healthy."

"Can, too." Nola walked up behind Marnie and grinned. "That dress would look better on you anyway. Go try it on."

Marnie whipped around and gave Nola a quick hug before darting into a dressing room. She yanked off her J. Crew denim skirt, sweater, and lace cami in mere seconds. When she came out of the dressing room, Nola was wearing a fisherman's cap and a trench coat over her clothes.

"Wow, you look fabulous," Nola said with a wide smile.

Marnie traipsed over to the full-length mirror again to check herself out. She loved the bold color. But it seemed so . . . status quo. So been-there, done-that. So eighth-grade Marnie.

"I don't know, I think I'm going to pick out something else," she said, twirling around so the bottom of the dress fluttered.

"Be my guest," Nola replied with a shrug.

In that moment, Marnie completely forgot that they were shopping for Nola's pseudo-date with Matt. Now, she was on a mission to find the perfect outfit for her birthday party next Saturday. As she was hunting, she was thinking about how Nola was going to react when she found out that she asked Lizette and company to come to her party, the one that Nola had been planning all summer long.

However, as she tried on the last ensemble, Marnie thought about how Lizette had reacted when she'd invited her. Marnie had mentioned, while Dane was still in earshot, that she was having a bash for her birthday next Saturday. Unfortunately, Dane had sprinted off when a friend of his called his name. As for Lizette, she'd just shrugged and said, "That's nice." Marnie had hoped for a bigger response from her. She would have killed for a reply like "Awesome! Tell me the deets because I don't want to miss it!" and would have settled for something like "Cool, can I come?" But all she had gotten was, "That's nice."

In fact, Lizette hadn't said much more than that to Marnie since they first met. She wasn't outright ignoring Marnie or anything. After all, yesterday Lizette had asked Marnie to read whatever was written on the bottle cap of her Snapple, *and* said, "Mmm-hmm," whenever Marnie interjected a comment during lunchtime conversation. But she hadn't gotten Lizette's undivided attention yet because the girl was way too preoccupied with Brynne and Grier.

Marnie was worried that she might never be truly welcomed into their group, but she had hoped that a great party would make the girls come around. And by that logic, Dane Harris would be that much easier to snag. The only thing left to do was get Nola on board with the plan.

Marnie emerged from the dressing room and shouted, "Ta-da!"

Nola doubled over with laughter, which was not the reaction Marnie was hoping for.

She frantically made her way to the mirror. Everything seemed fine — relatively speaking. Okay, so it wasn't something that she'd usually wear. But it was . . . avant-garde! Couldn't Nola see that?

"I think it's rather . . ." Marnie trailed off, trying to find the right adjective.

"Sorry, Marn," Nola said, giggling. "But I've just never seen you pair black-and-white-checkered capri leggings with an aqua-colored wrap shirt."

Marnie crossed her arms in front of her chest with

embarrassment. "I'm just trying something different, that's all."

Nola mumbled something as she strolled over to the shelves of hats.

"Speak up, Nol," Marnie said, a hint of annoyance lingering in her voice.

"Oh, I just, well," Nola stammered. "It kind of seems like something Lizette would wear."

Marnie stared at her reflection. It was true. The outfit looked as if it came straight from Lizette's walk-in closet. But she couldn't help but like the way she felt in it. It was the exciting sensation of being a whole new version of herself, combined with the thrilling feeling of being like someone else, someone other people envied. Marnie wished that she could explain this to Nola, but she felt that Nola wouldn't understand anyway. The girl was so stubborn about trivial things — like changing her shampoo — how could she comprehend Marnie's desire to change something as important as her image?

"I'll take that as a compliment then. Lizette has amazing style." Marnie adjusted her leggings, which were bunching up around her knees.

Nola walked over to the couch and flopped down again. "If you say so."

"It's not just me, Nol," Marnie argued. "Everyone thinks that Lizette is a trendsetter. We've only been in school for two days, and it's obvious that she decides what's in and what's out, not to mention *who's* in and who's out."

Nola stifled a yawn. "I know. You're right."

"I'm glad you agree," Marnie said, taking a seat next to Nola and bracing herself. "That's why I invited Lizette, Brynne, and Grier to come to the party next Saturday."

Marnie watched as Nola's neck became red and blotchy. *Only a couple more seconds until the hives,* Marnie thought.

"You're upset, aren't you?"

Nola shook her head. "Of course not. It's your birthday. You can invite whomever you want."

Marnie saw a tiny bump forming on Nola's collarbone. "It'll be oodles of fun, Nol. Trust me, all right?"

After a moment of awkward silence, Nola chuckled. "I just hope Lizette isn't mean to me because I killed her toe."

Marnie laughed and put her arm around Nola. "Don't worry. She's going to love you." *I hope.*

The skin on Nola's neck was starting to return to its normal hue. "Well, it looks like I need *two* outfits now. One for my 'big date' with Matt, and one for *the* birthday party of the year."

Marnie smiled as Nola shot up and galloped toward the sales rack. Although she appreciated Nola's enthusiasm, Marnie could tell that her friend was faking it. And that was okay.

For now, anyway.

Chapter 9

Three hours later, Nola came home without any shopping bags or new clothes. In fact, she was actually down one hoodie. Marnie's mom had taken them to Stewart's Ice Cream Shoppe for a (secret) hot fudge sundae, and Nola had hung the sweatshirt on the back of her chair. She'd forgotten all about it until she was dropped off at home. She called Stewart's immediately, but the manager said it was nowhere to be found.

This put her in a very bad mood. She loved that hoodie. The fleece on the inside was worn in just so. The sleeves were long enough to cover her hands when they got cold. She also liked to play with the hood strings. It calmed her anytime she was tense.

Only she was tense right now, and *some jerk had her hoodie!*

Nola walked into the kitchen, took a deep breath, and fetched herself a bottle of Vanilla Berry Hibiscus TeaNY. She shook it back and forth as she wandered into the living room, which was scattered with Xbox games, controller wires, and dirty plates. She was glad that Marnie had to go home for dinner, because the house was a mess.

Actually, that wasn't the only reason she was thankful Marnie wasn't there. Nola was still feeling stressed about this afternoon. First, Marnie had taken her to that strange store and started dressing like a crazy runway model, and then she'd dropped the bomb about her birthday. Nola went through a mental checklist of the things she had planned for next Saturday, and now she was worried that none of it would meet the Almighty Lizette's "In or Out" standards. Not only that, she was filling up with anxiety at the thought of having to *talk* to Lizette and those girls, let alone impress them with her party planning. It was so weird, feeling this unsettled when it came to Marnie.

Suddenly Dennis and Dylan popped up from behind the couch, armed with what looked like two aerosol cans.

"Ambush!" Dennis screamed and sprayed Nola with Silly String.

Dylan held his can up meekly, but did nothing.

"Get her, Dyl!" Dennis ordered when he saw his brother might be listening to his conscience.

In no time, Dylan complied.

As for Nola, she just stood there and took it like the loser big sister she was.

The boys got bored quickly, and within seconds they were gone. Nola peeled the Silly String off of her and stepped over the boys' wreckage toward her favorite spot in the living room — the window seat. It was the coziest place in the whole house, and Nola had claimed it as her necklace-making spot when she was about ten years old.

Underneath the long, rectangular seat cushion were four cabinets that held all of her supplies. Beads, cords, charms, wires, spools, pliers, zip bags — it was all nestled there, waiting for her to create another masterpiece.

Making jewelry was the only thing that gave Nola a sense of confidence. She knew she was good at it and, above all, she loved doing it. Although her dad always said it was a "cute girl hobby," it was way more than that to her. Nola was able to channel her nervous energy into something beautiful. Without her jewelry and Marnie, she wondered where she'd be.

Nola was about to open one of the cabinets and dip her hand into her bead drawer when her mom staggered into the room, half-asleep.

"Hey, sweetie," her mom said, rubbing her eyes.

"Nap time's over, huh?" Nola asked.

Her mom sat on the window seat and peered out at the front yard. "Yes, I have to go back to the hospital tonight. Double shift. Your dad's flying in on the red-eye, so can you watch the boys for a while?"

Nola groaned. "When are we getting a new baby-sitter, again?"

"We're interviewing, you know that." Her mom ran her fingers through Nola's hair.

"It's like you're always working."

Her mom stood up and stretched. "I know, honey. You won't have to do this for much longer. Just tonight and Tuesday."

Nola's eyes grew wide. "Mom, I can't on Tuesday. I have plans to study for a physics quiz with my classmate."

Mom can't argue with that. My schoolwork is at stake!

But Dr. James was not about to be swayed. "I feel terrible about this, but I can't possibly find anyone else before then. You're just going to have to study here at the house, Nola. I'm sorry."

Nola was so angry that she actually snarled, "Fine!" Then she dashed upstairs to her room and slammed the door.

It was really unlike Nola to be that rude to her mom, but she was feeling overwhelmed. And having to cancel her Tuesday-night plans really upset her. As she lay down on her bed and stared at the ceiling, she wondered if she was mad because she had to back out on Matt. If she had planned on studying with Marnie, would it have mattered as much?

Before she could give it much thought, she scrambled over to her PC and IMed him.

nolaj1994: *u there?*

His away-message flashed across the screen instantly.

mheatherly: *Rooney Fest, Deposit, NY*

Nola let out a sigh of relief when she realized he wasn't around, but at the same time, she noticed a gentle quivering in her stomach. It had to be nerves.

She just didn't want to make a bad impression on him, that's all.

But when she stared a little longer at his message, she couldn't help but imagine what stories Matt would share with her on Monday, and the quivering didn't stop.

Chapter 10

At 11:27 A.M. Monday morning, Marnie was sitting on a mat, stretching before her gym class. Unlike most girls, she didn't mind playing sports and getting so sweaty that her Cool Coconut–scented Teen Spirit Stick could barely handle the pressure. In fact, if Marnie didn't run at least three times a week, she felt like a garden slug. Plus, Erin had been a champion runner, and Marnie wondered if she could reach that level, too.

A petite girl with eyes the color of midnight tapped one of Marnie's pink Adidases with her gray Reebok. "Can you believe this get-up? These shorts are so 'I Love the Eighties Strikes Back in 3-D.'"

Marnie grinned. The girl was referring to their blue-and-white gym uniforms, which were the definition of retro. Only it wasn't a throwback to '80s fashion — the school board just hadn't updated the uniform since then. "I know. Polyester blends should be taken into the woods and shot dead."

"That's right. No mercy," the girl said. "I'm Iris Santos, by the way."

"Nice to meet you," she replied. "I'm Marnie Fitzpatrick."

She was waiting for the predictable "Are you Erin

Fitzpatrick's sister?" response, but before Iris could say anything else, Brynne Callaway strode into the gymnasium, rocking the lame uniform like nobody's business.

Brynne must have gotten the only baby tee, because everyone else was wearing a shirt long enough to be tucked into their shorts, while she had a small, taut strip of belly showing. Brynne's legs also had this glittery glow to them that screamed Jergens Soft Shimmer Lotion.

Marnie watched Brynne saunter past everyone and stand off in the corner, where she started to thoroughly examine her nails. Since Lizette and Grier weren't around, Brynne seemed as though she'd rather tend to her flaking cuticles than talk to the common folk. Even so, Marnie felt a twinge of sympathy for Brynne. Maybe Brynne felt the same way Nola did — scared and freaked out when she wasn't surrounded by the people she knew.

Marnie stood up and began to stretch her arms. She saw Brynne's eyes drift in her direction for a split second, so she decided to do the neighborly thing. "Hey, Brynne!" she called out, waving.

Iris shot up like something had stung her butt and slunk away to a crowd of girls sitting on the bleachers.

Brynne glanced over and looked Marnie up and down. "What?"

Marnie gulped. She hadn't thought of what to say after "Hey, Brynne." After an awkward pause, she finally replied, "Those boy-cut Sevens you wore yesterday were so cute."

Brynne revealed a hint of a smile and returned her gaze to her left ring finger. Apparently she knew how good she looked in her Sevens and didn't need reassurance from anyone.

Marnie didn't even bother checking to see if Iris and the rest of the girls had observed their awkward banter because she heard them snickering a few feet away. But soon it became clear that they were not laughing at her.

A rail-thin, gray-haired, wrinkly old lady dressed in a brown velour tracksuit and wearing silver Ray-Ban aviator sunglasses was standing before them. For a woman who should have been hunched over from massive bone loss, she had shockingly good posture. She was holding a neon-yellow soccer ball underneath her right arm and a bullhorn in her left hand, which she brought up to her mouth when she spoke.

"ALL RIGHT, GIRLS. UP AND AT 'EM!"

The bullhorn was at full volume, so everyone covered their ears.

"GET TOGETHER IN A GROUP SO I CAN CALL ROLL."

The class meandered about a bit before getting into formation.

"GIDDYUP, CHICKIES. THIS CLASS ISN'T FOR SLOWPOKES! DO YOU THINK I LIVED TO BE SEVENTY-EIGHT BY MOVING AT THE SPEED OF MOLASSES?"

Marnie rolled her eyes. It was just her luck to get a Centrum Silver–addicted drill sergeant for a gym teacher.

"MY NAME IS GRAMS. NOT MRS. GRAMS. NOT MS. GRAMS. NOT MISS GRAMS. JUST GRAMS. GOT IT?"

"Yes," the class muttered in unison.

"SPEAK UP, LASSIES. I'M DEAF IN ONE EAR."

"YES!" everyone screamed.

"MUCH BETTER. OKAY, HERE WE GO."

Marnie was patiently waiting for Grams to get to Fitzpatrick when someone tugged at the back of her T-shirt. It was Brynne, her eyes wide with worry and her shimmery skin gone pale. She leaned in and whispered, "Lizette isn't here yet."

Marnie's brow furrowed. "What?"

"She and Grier left during second-period study hall to grab a latte, but Lizette was supposed to be back by now." Brynne gnawed on her thumbnail as if it were covered in Nutella.

"MARNIE FITZPATRICK," Grams yelled.

"Here!" Marnie called without turning around.

"What do we do?" Brynne asked, her voice cracking.

We? Marnie couldn't believe this. Less than a minute ago Brynne would barely acknowledge her and now she was asking for *help?* Ew!

But then Marnie realized that this was the perfect opportunity to get on Lizette Levin's good side. She had to find a way to cover for the girl — and quick.

"LIZETTE LEVIN," Grams shouted. There was no answer. "I SAID, LIZETTE LEVIN!"

Suddenly, Marnie said, "Here."

Grams looked confused. "LITTLE GIRL, DIDN'T YOU SAY YOU WERE —" She glanced down at her clipboard and then back at the group. "SOMEONE ELSE?"

"No, ma'am," Marnie said with a totally straight face.

Grams studied the list once more and shrugged her shoulders. "WELL, THEN, MUST BE MY ALZHEIMER'S. MARGERY McSWEENEY!"

Marnie grinned as Grams continued on. She looked over at Brynne, who she hoped she'd impressed with her quick wit. But instead Brynne had a horrible scowl on her face, like she was mad that she hadn't thought of the trick herself. Marnie had no idea how to make nice with this girl.

After Grams finished roll, she instructed everyone

to run ten laps, but Marnie begged for the chance to go back to her gym locker and grab her good New Balance sneakers.

"JUST HUSTLE, LIZZY! HUSTLE!" was the positive, albeit excruciatingly loud, response.

As the other girls filed out of the gym, Marnie dashed back to the locker room, switched shoes, and ran through the gym toward the exit to the track. But she slowed down and peered over her shoulder when she heard a bunch of shouting coming from the boys' locker room.

"C'mon, guys! Leave me alone!"

"Where's your sense of humor, Dane?"

Marnie's ears perked up as if she were a German shepherd on K-9 patrol.

"Mess with the best, die like the rest!"

Marnie tiptoed closer and closer to the boys' locker room, hoping that she wouldn't be detected.

"Dudes, do *not* do this!"

All of a sudden, a boy came flying out of the locker room and fell onto the floor with a thud.

That boy was Dane Harris. And he was in his red-and-white-striped Hanes boxer shorts.

Wow. Wow. Wow. Wow.

When Dane got up and saw that Marnie was staring

at him, his cheeks turned red. He pressed against the locker room door with all his might, but it wouldn't budge.

Dane chuckled to himself and shook his head. Then he gave Marnie a heart-stopping smile. "Looks like I'm the victim of the oldest prank in the book."

Marnie grinned. Even during a humiliating moment, Dane seemed as composed and cool as he did behind the podium last Thursday. He was even easier on the eyes now. His damp hair was slicked back and the thin white T-shirt he had on showed the outline of his chest. His large hands were on his hips, as if he was posing for the cover of *GQ*.

"At least they didn't take *all* your clothes," Marnie said, raising an eyebrow.

Dane nearly hypnotized her with his laugh. "Yeah, well, they might come back for the rest."

Marnie batted her eyelashes as she pulled back her shoulders and tilted her head to the side. "I guess I'll have to protect you then."

"Really?" He crossed his arms over his chest and checked Marnie out from head to toe. "I think I'd like to see that."

The extra-loud screeching of a bullhorn echoed throughout the gym.

"WHEN I SAY *HUSTLE*, I *MEAN* HUSTLE!"

Marnie decided right then and there that she'd have to take Grams down. No doubt about it.

"I gotta go," she said, her body feeling warm all over.

"That's too bad." Dane ran one of his hands through his slick hair. "I'm defenseless now."

Marnie felt a tightness rise up into her throat, the same tightness she felt after she met Weston Briggs on the first day of eighth grade. She couldn't believe that was a year ago. How could she have gone that long without feeling this good?

"LET'S GO, LIZZY!"

Marnie immediately snapped out of her thoughts and said a hasty "see ya" to Dane. However, during her laps, the only thing on her mind was Weston and how they used to make out in the supply shed behind her house.

She didn't realize how fast she was running until she got a bad cramp in her side. She bent over, put her hands on her knees, and took some deep breaths until she pushed Weston back to the recesses of her memory, exactly where he belonged.

There were far more crush-worthy boys to focus on now.

Chapter 11

Nola was relieved that she had had an uneventful Monday morning. In fact, the only thing worth telling Iris and Evan about during lunch was that Miss Lucas had led the Pledge of Allegiance with her fly open. Nola felt as though Matt would have told the story much better, but he hadn't been in homeroom and he wasn't at lunch either. Not that Nola cared or anything.

Iris leaned over Nola and sniffed a few times. "Let me guess, Origins Ginger Essence, right?"

Nola nodded, hoping that Iris wouldn't notice that she had put on extra-thickening mascara and eaten ten Tic Tacs before coming to the cafeteria.

"She's an expert on fragrances," Evan said, keeping his eyes on his Sidekick.

"I can also smell nonsense from miles away," Iris shot back. "So stop dishing it out."

Nola grinned. Iris was really beginning to grow on her.

"So have you seen Matt around today?" Iris asked as she squirted a thick line of French's mustard onto her sauerkraut-covered hot dog.

Weird. The second Iris said his name, Nola's mouth became as dry as sand. She grabbed her can of A&W and chugged it.

"No," she replied with a tiny hiccup.

Evan put his Sidekick in his pocket and turned his attention to the mound of Tater Tots on his plate. He popped three in his mouth. "Probably on his way back from Rooney."

Iris grabbed some ketchup and poured it over Evan's tots. He didn't seem amused. "I can't believe Matt went up there again. The boy has lost his mind."

Nola took another sip of her root beer. "What's Rooney Fest, anyway?"

Evan ripped open some salt packets and emptied the contents onto Iris's hot dog. He chuckled when she growled at him. "You mean, what *was* Rooney Fest."

Iris turned to Nola. "It was this bluegrass musical festival that took place in this muddy field over in Deposit, like, during the eighties. Matt and a couple of his freak music-camp friends went up there last year to try and revive it."

Nola couldn't hide the smile on her face. "Did it work?"

"No way," Iris said, chuckling. "Some deadbeat played the harmonica for a few hours and they all got attacked by mosquitoes."

Evan threw a ketchup-covered Tater Tot at Iris and missed by an inch. "At least the guy has a dream."

Iris sneered at Evan. "You want me to ram this dog down your throat?"

Nola laughed while Evan rolled his eyes and got out his Sidekick.

"That's what I thought," Iris said triumphantly. "So, Nola, what's up with you tonight? Do you want to hit Three Arts? They just got a new shipment of second-hand books."

Nola gave Iris a half grin. She had already planned on meeting up with Marnie after school. "Actually, I'm hanging out with my best friend later on." As soon as she said that, she swallowed hard — was it mean not to invite Iris along?

"That's cool. Who's your best friend?" she asked.

Nola paused for a moment. It was strange hearing somebody ask her that. In middle school, everyone could plainly see that she and Marnie were inseparable. "Oh, um, Marnie Fitzpatrick."

"No kidding." Iris raised an eyebrow. "Never would have guessed that."

"Why not?"

Iris shrugged her shoulders. "She just seems really . . . fake, you know, like Lizette, Brynne, and the rest of their crew."

Nola's body temperature shot up several degrees. *Fake? Like Lizette and Brynne?* "She's *not* fake, Iris. And she doesn't even know those other girls."

It seemed as though Iris could sense that she had touched a nerve, so she patted Nola on the back. "Sorry, I didn't mean anything by it. I just thought since Marnie was chillin' with Brynne during gym class, and she covered for Lizette, I assumed that they were tight. My bad."

Nola swallowed hard. She had no idea what any of that meant, but it didn't matter. Iris had mistaken Marnie for a member of Lizette's group, and somehow couldn't believe Nola and Marnie were best friends. How could either of those things even be possible?

"I'll be right back," Nola said as she grabbed her bag and shot up from the table. She bolted out the cafeteria door and down the hallway to the girls' bathroom.

She felt a shot of air-conditioning wash over her when she entered, which was good, considering that she was seconds away from a mini-panic attack. But the second Nola saw Grier Hopkins reapplying her mascara in the mirror, she got even tenser. She had no choice but to take her melodrama into a stall so that Grier wouldn't see her transform into the Human Hive.

Nola abruptly turned to her left and pushed on the

door to the last stall. But instead of finding a place to hide, she found Lizette Levin.

"Oh my God, *get out of here!*" Lizette shouted.

Nola retreated faster than a crowd at a K-Fed concert. "I'm sorry! I had no idea you were in there!"

Lizette slammed the door shut. "Grier, you were supposed to be holding this closed for me!"

Grier became flustered, mindlessly smearing mascara across her left cheek. "I just turned my back for a second! It's not my fault!" she cried.

"What*ever*! People are supposed to knock first. Are you retarded or something?"

Nola figured this remark was aimed at her. "I . . . I . . . ." She couldn't get any more syllables out.

"She didn't mean it, Zee," Grier whimpered.

"Yeah, right." Lizette's voice was pinched and gravelly at the same time.

"I said I was sorry," Nola repeated. She knew she was on the verge of crying, so she darted out of the bathroom and into the empty band practice room, which was only a few feet away.

As she sunk into a chair near a bassoon, Nola frantically text-messaged Marnie.

HELP!

Within seconds, Nola's phone rang.

"What's wrong?" was the first thing Marnie said.

Nola wiped at her runny nose. "I accidentally walked in on Lizette when she was going to the bathroom. It was so embarrassing. And she seemed *really* mad!"

"You're kidding, right?"

"Does it *sound* like I'm kidding?"

"Um, no," Marnie replied. "Where are you?"

"In the band practice room." Nola sniffled. "Where are you?"

"Locker room. Just got out of gym. I have lunch in a few minutes, though, so maybe we could meet up real quick before your next class."

"Okay," Nola mumbled.

"It's going to be all right, Nol. See you in a bit," Marnie said.

But when they hung up, Nola felt anything but all right.

Nola made her way to her next class in a complete daze. Although Marnie had been able to calm her down somewhat during their quick chat, Nola was unable to quit thinking about what Iris had said at lunch or what had happened with Lizette in the bathroom. The incidents haunted her during the first few minutes of physics, too. In fact, she didn't even realize that Matt had been tossing crumpled-up pieces of loose leaf at her until one hit her on the forehead.

Nola looked up and saw Matt giving her a cute little salute, which lightened her mood almost instantly. He was wearing a black T-shirt over a white waffle-knit Henley, sandblasted jeans, and a pair of Doc Martens. His hair was tousled as usual and the white wires from his iPod earbuds were dangling around his neck.

Clearly, someone had made it back from Rooney Fest in time for physics. Mr. Newkirk, Poughkeepsie Central's youngest and coolest teacher, cleared his throat and loosened his necktie before addressing the class. "Okay, folks, you'll need to partner up for this problem, so find someone who won't bring your grade down and check out page forty-five in your workbook."

Matt picked up his things without hesitation and moved over to Nola's side of the classroom. Nola was able to forget about her crises long enough to take her hair out of its ponytail holder. She shook her head slightly so her pale brown locks fell down around her shoulders. She quickly ran her hands through some strands to get all the knots out. Matt slid into the seat next to her before she had a chance to reach for her Tic Tacs.

"Hey there," he said, lightly nudging her on the arm. "How was your weekend?"

At the moment, the only thing Nola could recall was their IM exchange Friday and how her mom had told her she had to babysit tomorrow.

"Fine," Nola replied.

Matt stared into her eyes. "Care to elaborate on that?"

Nola immediately glanced away and began clicking her pen. How was she going to cancel on him without looking like a complete idiot? "It was pretty boring, actually."

"Well, I had the best weekend in the history of week-ends." Matt dug through his corduroy messenger bag as if he was hoping to strike gold at the bottom of it. "How awesome is this?"

Matt pulled out his Sony digital camera and leaned in closer so that Nola could see the viewfinder. As he pushed a bunch of buttons, she studied his hands. His long, thin fingers moved speedily, like they instinctively knew where they were going and what they were doing. She also liked the smell of him: definitely Axe body spray.

Suddenly a movie clip popped up on the screen. Nola smiled as she watched Matt play bass guitar in a muddy field with three other guys, who were most likely the music-camp freaks Iris mentioned at lunch. Even though they weren't very good, Nola could tell that Matt had talent just by the way he closed his eyes and concentrated as he plucked away at the heavy strings.

After the video stopped, Matt turned to Nola and smiled widely. "I know. We're really bad."

Nola laughed. "You're not bad. You're a . . . work in progress."

"Well put." Matt grinned. "It was a blast though. Five more people came than last year. I swear, by two thousand and ten, Rooney Fest will be on the map again."

"I'm sure you're right." Nola saw Mr. Newkirk making his rounds so she opened her book and flipped to page forty-five. Matt noticed as well so he followed Nola's lead.

"So do you want to meet up at the library tomorrow or do you want to come over to my house? I make killer double fudge brownies," he whispered. "Duncan Hines puts in most of the grunt labor though. Poor guy never gets the credit he deserves."

Nola felt so terrible for what she was about to do, and she couldn't figure out why. This wasn't a big deal at all, but still, her stomach felt as if someone was break-dancing in it. She kept her eyes on her book and steadied herself before lowering the boom. "Sorry, Matt. I have to watch my little brothers tomorrow night."

There was a slight pause. Nola's heart was pumping so hard she was sure Matt could hear it.

"No problem. Some other time," he finally said.

Nola exhaled and closed her eyes. She wanted to look over at him and say "thanks for understanding," but Matt had already started applying the laws of physics to the word problem on page forty-five. She watched as he scribbled diligently in his workbook, pushing up his sleeves and revealing his blue rubber wristband again.

After class was over, Nola found herself smiling when she realized that "RF" stood for "Rooney Fest," and wishing that "some other time" meant "soon."

Chapter 12

"So I hear that you've stolen my identity," Lizette Levin said as she cornered Marnie in the lunch line ten minutes later.

Marnie gulped and edged by Lizette so that she could grab a minicarton of one-percent milk from the refrigerator. She'd hoped that Lizette would be stoked that someone had protected her from the wrath of Sergeant Grams, but the strained expression on Lizette's flawless face suggested the exact opposite. And given that Nola had just ambushed her in the bathroom, Marnie figured that Lizette was most likely in witch mode.

"Um, yeah, I kind of did," Marnie replied, her hands shaking so much that her plastic tray was wobbling.

Lizette toyed with the zipper on her black leather bomber jacket, which she was wearing over an ultra-feminine lace cami and floral-print bubble skirt. "I don't remember saying you could do that," she finally snapped.

"I know, but —" Marnie could feel her palms sweating.

Just then Brynne appeared, and she wasn't scowling anymore. Her glossy lips had turned into this wide, sinister smirk, as if she was happy to see Marnie with her back against the Snapple machine.

Brynne chomped on a wad of gum and eyed the soup of the day with disgust. "I told her to mind her own business, Lizette, but, like, she was just *begging* for attention."

Marnie's mouth fell open. *What a psycho!*

"Is that so?" Lizette asked crossly.

Marnie glanced over at Brynne, who was now talking with a cute boy. "I was just trying to cover for you. I didn't mean to upset you or anything."

Within seconds, Lizette's demeanor softened and her sneer turned into a smile. She started laughing as if she'd just watched a lost episode of *Chappelle's Show*. "I was only playing."

Marnie had no idea what to make of Lizette's schizoid mood, so she stood there, motionless.

"You totally saved my life." Lizette put her arm around Marnie and gave her a little squeeze. "Thank you."

Marnie was still completely baffled, but she managed to muster up a halfhearted chuckle. "No problem."

Lizette led Marnie to their regular table, where Grier was eating carrots out of a small sandwich bag. Lizette sat down in between Marnie and Grier. When Brynne showed up moments later, she didn't seem pleased with the seating arrangements at all. Her cheeks turned pink as she sat next to Grier and heaved a big sigh of frustration.

If looks could kill, I'd be dead and in the trunk of Brynne's car right now, Marnie thought.

Lizette took out a Zone bar from her jacket pocket and began to unwrap it. "So tell me everything," she said excitedly to Marnie.

Grier stopped nibbling long enough to add, "I can't *wait* to hear this."

As for Brynne, she was far from amused. "Puh-lease, all she did was say 'here' when the gym teacher called Lizette's name. I mean, the lady is a zillion years old. She wasn't that hard to fool."

Lizette rolled her eyes. "If it was so easy, Brynne, why didn't *you* do it?"

It was quite obvious that there was tension in the ranks as Brynne bowed her head in submission. Marnie couldn't be more pleased with the way things were going.

"It wasn't a big deal," Marnie said modestly. "I just didn't want you to get in trouble."

Grier put her tiny freckled hand over her heart. "That's *so* sweet."

"Well, I definitely owe you one," Lizette said before biting into some chocolate-covered protein goodness.

Marnie looked over at Brynne, who was sulking so much she might have been straining a few muscles. "No, you don't."

"Yeah, I do." Lizette reached into her other jacket pocket and pulled out a plaid Kate Spade mini wallet. Marnie was almost blinded by the sparkly gold hue of Lizette's American Express card. "How about a shopping spree after school? Daddy just paid off the balance with his D&A check."

Grier applauded gleefully and Brynne eked out a pitiful, "Fine."

Lizette turned to Marnie. "That leaves you."

Marnie bit her lip. Yesterday she'd invited Nola over to her house to watch a few episodes of the first season of *Veronica Mars* on DVD that afternoon. She knew that bailing on Lizette for this reason would drop her down into the Minors quickly.

On the other hand, asking Nola to come along might be a disaster. Nola would act all awkward and weird, and Lizette probably wouldn't want to spend time with the girl who'd walked in on her in the bathroom, unless Marnie severely kissed up.

However, if Marnie said she could go, Brynne might tear her to shreds with her professionally whitened teeth.

This is so confusing!

"It'll be way fun," Grier reassured her.

"*Waaaaay* fun," Lizette chimed in.

Another creepy death stare from Brynne.

After a few more seconds of deliberation, Marnie considered once again what Erin Fitzpatrick might have said in this situation.

"I'm in," she replied.

And with that, Brynne excused herself from the table and stormed off, leaving Marnie to wonder what the other girl was up to.

When the dismissal bell rang at 2:58, Marnie ran to her locker at lightning speed. She had told Lizette that she'd meet her on the school steps, where Lizette's father would be waiting in his Acura SUV. After she threw a few books into her purple, patent-leather oversized tote, she stopped to check out her T-zone in the small square mirror that was glued to the inside of her locker door.

Yikes, shiny chin.

Marnie needed some loose powder ASAP, so she reached up and tried to grab her makeup bag off the top shelf. A long, lean arm suddenly extended above her head and a large hand took her pink Caboodle right out of her grasp. She turned around and saw Dane Harris, in all of his button-down, khaki-pants, perfectly coiffed glory.

Dane unzipped the bag and began looking through it. "Anything good in here?"

Marnie was caught off guard, but not enough for the cute dimples in his cheeks to go unnoticed. "You should really give that back to me," she said, smiling so wide that her gums were probably showing.

"Or what?" Dane put the bag behind his back and grinned mischievously.

Marnie raised an eyebrow. "Or you'll be sorry."

Dane laughed and took a step backward. "I don't know. Your threat wasn't very convincing."

Her smile was even wider now. Dane Harris was totally flirting with her! How could this day get any better?

"Don't let my appearance fool you," she said, approaching him slowly. "I'm dangerous."

Dane's eyes brightened. "That's more like it." He took Marnie's right hand in his, brought the bag from behind his back, and put it in Marnie's possession. His fingers gently grazed her skin as he let go.

"Thanks," she said, a little breathlessly.

Dane took a quick look at his Fossil watch and shook his head. "I gotta go. The Key Club is meeting in two minutes."

"That's okay, I'm leaving with Lizette in a few secs." Marnie hoped that Dane would consider this piece of info a plus.

"Really? Well, stay out of trouble," he said with a wink. "See ya around." Then he sprinted down the hall, hopping over a stray recycling bin before turning the corner and running out of Marnie's view.

She was still in a daze when she felt someone come up behind her.

It was Nola, all smiles and sunshine for a change.

"Was that who I think it was?" she asked excitedly.

Marnie looked at the clock at the end of the hall, which read 3:01. "Um, yeah." She dove into her makeup bag, pulled out her Clinique compact, and blotted her chin rapidly.

"Aren't you psyched?"

The only thing on Marnie's mind right now was that Lizette was waiting for her out front. "I am," she said, slinging her tote over her shoulder.

Nola's mouth puckered up as if she'd bit into a lemon. "What's wrong?"

"Nothing, I'm just in a hurry."

"Are you sure you're not mad at me about the bathroom thing?" Nola asked solemnly.

"Of course not. You didn't do anything wrong. I'm sure Lizette has cooled off and realized that, too."

Marnie let out a sigh of frustration. Nola's neurotic side was a bit much to take sometimes.

"Good, because I'd hate to let today's little snafu ruin Veronica night."

Marnie's heart clenched tightly in her chest. She'd put that plan of theirs out of her mind once she'd said yes to Lizette.

"I packed all my supplies, too." Nola opened up her canvas book bag to reveal plastic Gladware filled with colorful glass and plastic beads. "I figured you might want to learn some tricks of the trade."

Now Marnie's legs were going numb. How could she possibly flake out on Nola? Then again, how could she possibly flake out on Lizette? There was only one solution. She'd bring Nola along and face the consequences. After all, if there was a chance Lizette might come to her birthday party on Saturday, Ms. Major would have to hang out with Nola then. Marnie might as well get the initial awkwardness over with.

She inhaled deeply and began. "Actually, Nol, Lizette asked me to go shopping with her and the girls after school."

Nola's face flushed red. "Oh."

"I'm sorry, I totally spaced on the Veronica thing." Marnie almost winced as the little white lie escaped her lips.

"Whatever," Nola said. "We can do it on Wednesday."

Marnie put a sisterly arm around Nola. "Why don't you come with us?"

"Nah, that's okay. You go ahead."

"Come on, it'll be a blast. Maybe Lizette will buy us all diamonds or something. You don't want to miss out on that, do you?"

"Marn, I doubt she'd buy me anything right now," Nola snorted, rolling her eyes. "Besides, I'm all shopped out from Saturday. Have a good time."

"I'll IM you later, okay?"

"Sure. I can't wait to hear all about it," Nola said, with a hint of sarcasm in her voice.

Marnie knew she kind of deserved that. Backing out on Nola was an awful thing to do. But when she thought about it on the way out to the front steps, she realized that she actually *wanted* to go with Lizette and her friends. She and Nola had hung out almost every day for eight years. Was it wrong to want to try something else on for size?

Marnie wasn't sure, but as she piled into Mr. Levin's tricked-out ride with Lizette, Brynne, and Grier, she figured she could forget about Nola's problems for a while.

Monday, Sept 10, 10:05 P.M.

marniebird: *u still up?*
nolaj1994: *y*
marniebird: *i had soooo much fun! but i was soooo bummed b/c u weren't there. u should have come*
nolaj1994: *maybe next time. so did LL buy u diamonds or what?*
marniebird: *not exactly. her dad dropped us off at the galleria and we spent hours trying on clothes and talking*
nolaj1994: *cool*
marniebird: *and then LL got me this awesome denim jacket @ sally's*
nolaj1994: *wait, u guys stole a jacket from sally applebaum?*
marniebird: *hahahaha. no, that's what LL calls the salvation army on main street. it was our last stop*
nolaj1994: *oh*
marniebird: *anyway, it was only $5. and it has message buttons all over it! u know, like ones that say "groovy man" and "prayn4peace"*
nolaj1994: *u r a big fan of those*
marniebird: *LL says the jacket is fierce*
nolaj1994: *fierce?*

marniebird: *yeah, it's her catchphrase. She luvs* America's Next Top Model

nolaj1994: *that's kind of dumb*

marniebird: *really? i think it's cute*

nolaj1994: *no, dumb*

marniebird: ☺ *well i luv this jacket. perfect for fall, goes with everything. luv luv luv it*

nolaj1994: *nice*

marniebird: *so any more news on the MH front?*

nolaj1994: *i canceled our study date*

marniebird: *what?*

nolaj1994: *have 2 babysit*

marniebird: *i'm sorry. but it's prob 4 the best anyway*

nolaj1994: *why?*

marniebird: *don't get upset. i heard he was kind of a misfit and suspended from school B4, etc.*

nolaj1994: *who told u that? LL?*

marniebird: *she would know, they went 2 arlington 2gether*

nolaj1994: *so, she could b lying*

marniebird: *no way. she's telling the truth. besides, why would she lie?*

nolaj1994: *i dunno. it's just hard 2 believe, that's all*

marniebird: *i guess*

nolaj1994: *thx for telling me though*

marniebird: *np*
nolaj1994: *gotta get 2 bed, tired*
marniebird: *me 2*
nolaj1994: *LYLAS*
marniebird: *LYLAS*

Chapter 13

On Tuesday evening, Nola hovered over the kitchen stove and stirred a big pot full of Velveeta Shells & Cheese. She fixed this taboo dinner for Dylan and Dennis whenever she wanted them to be on their best behavior. And tonight was one of those nights. Nola wanted to spend most of the evening preparing for Marnie's birthday party without interruption, so bribing her little brothers with processed cheese sauce seemed like the smart thing to do.

This sure smells good, she thought as the steam rose up and moistened her face. She wiped her hands on her Aéropostale jean shorts, put the wooden spoon on the counter, and sat at the table so she could study the Marnie-inspired to-do list that she'd written a few weeks ago.

1) Go to Hobby House and buy glass beads, stone chips, hematite tubes, and coiled memory wire, for M's bracelet.
2) Stop at Sprout Creek Market for ingredients for chocolate layer cake and homemade vanilla ice cream.

3) Buy piñata, sombrero, confetti poppers, plastic limbo bar, and noisemakers at House of Cards.
4) Download Marnie's favorite KT Tunstall and OutKast songs off iTunes for party playlist.
5) Borrow D&D's Xbox and rent *Dance Dance Revolution* from Blockbuster.
6) Rip a copy of *New York Minute*.

Once she finished reviewing the list, she sighed deeply. *Limbo bar? Dance Dance Revolution?* These ideas had seemed great before, but now Nola feared that she was planning the weakest fourteenth birthday party in all of Poughkeepsie. Marnie used to love doing silly stuff on her birthday, like having hula-hoop contests in the backyard or playing Pin the Tail on Pikachu. Even last year, Marnie insisted that they bob for Granny Smith apples, which had been fun until Nola chipped a bicuspid.

Over the years, Nola had suspected that Marnie enjoyed these activities because no one else was around to witness her participation — money was always tight at the Fitzpatrick household, so all of Marnie's parties had been held at home and the invitee list was usually held to five of Marnie's friends. But from the way Marnie had acted over Lizette and the junky, hand-me-down, wannabe vintage denim jacket, Nola doubted that Marnie would want to do the Running Man in front of any Majors.

Nola reached into her pocket, pulled out her phone, and checked to see if there was a new text message in her inbox. *Nope, nothing.* Nola had sent Marnie several texts about the party and all of them had gone unanswered. She scrolled through some old messages from the summer and giggled. Marnie was a master at squeezing an insane amount of info into the smallest amount of letters, numbers, and symbols possible. Not only that, Marnie could text without even looking down at her phone. However, she also used to write Nola back within minutes of receiving a message. But that wasn't the case today.

Another thing that was weird: the comment Marnie had made about Matt last night. Where had *that* come from? Sure, Nola barely knew the guy, and she didn't know if he *was* a misfit who had been suspended or not. The thought of it being true bothered her, but it bothered her even more that Marnie seemed so quick to believe Lizette rather than give Matt, a person Nola liked and vouched for, the benefit of the doubt.

Nola set her phone down on the table and resumed her position back at the stove. She fished out a piece of cheesy macaroni with the wooden spoon to see if it was ready. The shell practically melted in her mouth, so she'd overcooked it, but considering that Dennis and Dylan's usual supper involved steamed broccoli, she didn't think they'd mind too much.

She picked up her two-way Motorola radio, which was lying on top of the fridge, and paged her two brothers, but they didn't respond. She walked to the back door and peered outside the nearby window. They didn't seem to be in the yard. But Dennis and Dylan were professional pains in the rear, so there was a good chance they were hiding out there, waiting for Nola to emerge so they could assault her with their Super Soaker Triple Aggressors.

She tried once again. "Dennis and Dylan, dinner is ready. Time to come home. Over."

The only reply she received was in the form of a loud clap of thunder.

Great, just great, Nola thought. *Those twerps are going to get drenched.*

She opened the back door and stepped out onto the deck. The wind was picking up and blowing leaves and twigs off the trees. Dark gray clouds scattered across the sky. A storm was only minutes away.

Nola made her descent on the stairs very carefully, listening for any sudden sounds or movements that might accompany a sneak attack. A grin came across her face when she heard footsteps coming from alongside the house. This couldn't be more perfect. She scampered over to the corner of the house and leaned back, waiting for the right moment to strike. As soon as she saw a figure come into view, she jumped out, screamed, "AAAAHHHHH!" at the top of her lungs, and pushed the person to the ground.

"Yikes!" someone yelped.

Even though the sound of earsplitting thunder was echoing all around her, Nola knew that that wasn't the voice of either Dennis or Dylan.

When she took a close look at her victim, she could see that it was a very stunned Matt Heatherly.

Nola closed her eyes and prayed that the lords of the universe would put an end to her suffering by striking her dead with a bolt of lightning. At least then she wouldn't have to endure this humiliation.

"Oh . . . um . . . I didn't know it was you," was the only thing she could blurt out.

Matt got up and brushed himself off, chuckling. "I'm almost afraid to ask who you were expecting."

Nola smiled. Leave it to Matt to be completely unaffected by her dorkiness — and incredibly cute. "I thought you were one of my little brothers."

"Understood." He picked a yellow leaf out of his hair and flicked it at Nola.

"What are you doing here?" she asked, her voice rising above the roaring thunder.

Matt reached into his beat-up messenger bag and pulled out a physics workbook that had NOLA JAMES written on the cover. "I guess I grabbed yours by mistake yesterday."

"Oh, thanks." When he handed over the book, Nola could feel herself deflate a bit. She'd hoped that he'd come over for some other reason, but apparently he was just being a physics class do-gooder. However, that fact did make it less believable that he was a troublemaker.

"No problem." He set his bag on the ground, put his hands in his jeans pockets, and leaned back on his heels. "Hope you don't mind me tracking you down. I just remembered you were stuck home tonight, so . . ." His voice trailed off.

Nola caught herself gawking at the heart-shaped grenade on his Green Day T-shirt and promptly glanced away. "That's okay."

Matt made his way toward the tire swing that hung from the oak tree Nola's father had planted seven years ago. He put his hands on the rope and hoisted himself up so that he was swaying back and forth while standing on the bottom half of the tire. "You have a really nice house. You know, it only took me about twenty minutes to ride over on my bike."

Nola raised an eyebrow. *That's a long way to go just to give me my book, isn't it?*

She would have dwelled on this idea more, if she hadn't been hit in the back of the head with a water balloon. Nola whipped around to see Dennis and Dylan standing at the top of the deck stairs, laughing hysterically.

"Bull's-eye!" Dennis shouted and high-fived Dylan.

Usually Nola would just ignore this ugly display of childishness, but *usually* there wasn't a boy watching her get humiliated by a couple of nine-year-olds. Therefore, she decided that this called for extreme measures.

"You guys are *dead!*" she shrieked, running up the stairs with a raised fist. Dennis taunted her by making a face, then grabbed Dylan by the shirt collar and dragged him into the house through the back door. Nola got there just as the boys slammed it shut and locked it. She was yanking on the doorknob furiously when Matt came up behind her.

"Everything okay?"

Nola tried to play it cool. "Of course. This is just one of our little games."

Matt laughed out loud. "Looks like fun. Can I play on your team?"

Nola covered her reddening face with her hands. This was beyond embarrassing. And it was about to get worse. She felt a drop of water fall on her shoulder. Then another. Then ten more. Within seconds, heavy rain was showering down from the sky.

Matt's eyes narrowed when he saw the boys pointing and laughing at them through the window. "I take it back. This game *isn't* all that fun."

"I know," Nola growled.

"Should we try the front door?" Matt asked, brushing damp strands of hair from his forehead.

Nola stared into Dennis's and Dylan's beady little eyes as she felt her black tank top soaking through. "Run to the front of the house as fast as you can, okay? I'll be right behind you."

"Got it." Matt leaped over the railing of the deck and landed on the ground three feet below. Then he sprinted around the side of the house before she even made it down the stairs.

Nola's flip-flops were sliding off her feet with every wet step, so she was only able to manage a slow jog. But much to her surprise, when she got to the front porch, the door was wide open. She dashed inside the house and shut it behind her. The moment she turned around, she started laughing so hard that her sides hurt.

Matt had Dennis and Dylan down on the floor, in headlocks, begging for mercy.

"I changed my mind again," he said, laughing along with Nola. "This game rocks."

Suddenly Nola was covered in a million goose bumps. She knew her skin was probably reacting to the cold rain, but when her eyes met Matt's, her breathing became quick and shallow, so she immediately looked away.

Chapter 14

Marnie was sitting in movie theater C at Regal Cinemas with her feet up on the chair in front of her, and her new favorite denim jacket wrapped around her bare legs. It was t-minus ten minutes until the previews started rolling and the latest Will Ferrell movie appeared on the screen, but she was already on the edge of her seat with excitement.

Ever since Lizette had taken her shopping yesterday, Marnie's mood had shifted between way-worried and super excited about every thirty seconds, depending on whether Lizette was being ambivalent or nice to her. Still, being tight with Lizette and her friends was worth experiencing the symptoms of bipolar disorder.

Besides, if she made it through the drama, the Era of Erin might turn into the Marnie Millennium.

Now, if there was only a way to get Nola in on this before it's too late, she thought. Marnie had gotten three text messages from her friend in the past two hours, but she'd been too tied up eating stuffed grape leaves with Lizette to reply. She knew that it wasn't cool to stiff her best friend, but at the same time, she was scared that if she seemed the slightest bit distracted, Lizette might think she wasn't grateful to be there or something. The solution was to bring everyone together — that had been the plan in the first place after all. Marnie just had to find the right approach and hope that Lizette had forgotten about the bathroom episode (which wasn't very likely) or had a Pope-sized compassionate side (even more unlikely).

"Tucker might be flashier, but there's no possible way he's better-looking than Dane," Brynne said, horrified.

The girls were having a little debate. The topic was *Who's hotter:* preppie demigod and all-around amazing Dane Harris, or Tucker McFadden, the most notable burnout in the junior class, who just happened to have more money than Donald Trump? Marnie couldn't get a word in edgewise, so she kept busy by counting how many times Lizette said the word *fierce*. She was up to twelve.

Grier finally realized that she was indoors, so she took off her extra-large, bug-eyed Dior sunglasses and placed them on top of her red mane. "I agree with Brynne. Tucker may be a trust-fund kid, but he's —"

"As greasy as an oil spill?" Marnie cut in.

Lizette let out a huge snort of a laugh, Grier giggled, and Brynne had no reaction at all. (*Shocker,* Marnie thought.)

"Exactly." Lizette readjusted her flamingo-pink off-the-shoulder sweatshirt so that it was showing maximum skin. "But shouldn't Dane just change his name to *Dull* already? He's cute and all, but I wouldn't be shocked if the guy tried to coordinate his outfit with the color of his Diamondback."

This time, everyone laughed except for Marnie. How could Lizette trash Dane? Did she really think he was dull? Marnie went over their two encounters in her head and she couldn't stop her heart from fluttering.

Then she thought about what Lizette had said about Matt last night. They had all squeezed into a handicapped fitting room at American Eagle to try on miniskirts when Brynne started going off on all the "dirt bags" who worked there. Lizette had laughed and said with great authority, "They're probably all friends with Matt Heatherly." Then she'd gone on to talk about a string of rumors regarding his frequent, mysterious trips to the principal's office and his weeklong suspension from Arlington.

Still, Nola had seemed so certain that Lizette was wrong about Matt, and now that Lizette had made fun of Dane, too, Marnie was wondering if she was a reliable source after all.

Lizette tugged mindlessly at her nude fishnets. "Neither of them are as fine as Sawyer Lee, though."

Then again, maybe she was the most reliable source in the northern hemisphere.

"*You* like Sawyer Lee?" Marnie sounded shocked,

but she could hardly knock the girl's taste. She had day-dreamed that Sawyer and his Krooked skateboard would show up at her house for years. Until Dane came into the picture, that is.

"'Pine after' is more like it," Brynne put in with a wicked grin.

Lizette wasn't amused. "Ugh. You have that so wrong. It's pretty obvious from how Sawyer stares in my direction during homeroom that he pines after *me*. I'm just waiting to give *him* the green light."

Marnie grinned. Even though Lizette was interested in the now number two guy on Marnie's Crush List, she just couldn't get any cooler. Besides, if Lizette thought Sawyer was worthy enough to "pine after," maybe that meant she and Marnie had a lot in common.

"The movie is about to start," Grier said, checking her watch. "I better go to the ladies'." She grabbed her brown leather bag and left the theater in a hurry.

Marnie's hands immediately got clammy. Grier was a nice girl, and whenever she was around, Marnie felt a little less vulnerable. But now Lizette was the only thing between Marnie and Brynne's mean glares.

"Do you want anything to eat?" Brynne asked while undoing a button on her Ralph Lauren long-sleeved polo shirt dress, which looked a size too small.

"I'd love some popcorn," Marnie said cheerfully.

"I wasn't talking to *you*," Brynne huffed.

Marnie was so taken aback that she flinched. "Sorry."

Brynne cleared her throat and began again. "Lizette, can I get you something? Twizzlers? Junior Mints?"

Lizette shrugged. "I don't care. Whatever."

"Okay, be right back." Brynne darted out of the theater as quick as a ball runner at the U.S. Open.

Marnie was alone with Lizette now. She had a feeling that if she said something great she could make a lasting impression, something that would make her sister, Erin, green with envy. But Brynne's harsh dis had totally thrown off her game. Marnie was so anxious that she could feel herself sweating through her multi-layered Gap T-shirts.

"So," Lizette said, turning to face Marnie. "Isn't it, like, your birthday this weekend?"

Marnie's rock-bottom low instantly shot up to a Rocky-Mountain high. *Lizette Levin remembered my birthday!*

"Yeah, on Saturday," she replied calmly.

"Sweet." Lizette took out a comb from her tiny black belt bag and tried to run it through her messy mop of bed-head hair. "Where's the party again?"

And with that question, Marnie was back down at rock bottom. Here she was, talking with a Major about her birthday plans, and all she could think about was how she'd look like a Minor — or something even worse — if she told Lizette the truth.

All of a sudden Marnie felt her cell phone vibrating in her shorts pocket. She pulled it out and looked at the LCD screen.

1 MESSAGE RECEIVED

"One sec," she said as she opened her in-box.

A text from Nola.

MATT IS OVER. HE HAS GREAT IDEAS FOR UR B-DAY! :)

Marnie now sank below rock bottom. How could she even consider — even for a millisecond — *not* telling Lizette that her best friend in the whole world was planning her special day? She'd be crazy to do something that despicable.

She turned off her phone, put it back in her pocket, and took a deep breath. "The party's at my house, actually."

Back from the bathroom, Grier skipped down the aisle and sat next to Marnie. "Ooh! There's a party? Cool beans."

Marnie felt a bit safer now that Grier was nearby. "Yes, for my birthday."

"Oh, that's right. Happy birthday!" Grier gave Marnie a hug.

"Thanks."

"So who's going to be there?" Lizette returned the comb to her belt bag and zipped it closed.

Marnie swallowed hard. *Say it. Say it. Say. It.* "Just me and my best friend. She's putting the party together."

Lizette gave her a blank stare. "Huh. Who's that?"

"Nola James."

Grier gasped.

That can't be good, Marnie thought.

"Nola *James?*" Lizette's face contorted into something inhuman.

"Yes," Marnie stated, her voice cracking. "I guess you know her, right?"

"Oh, I *know* who she is," Lizette snapped, her eyes fiery.

This is seriously *not good.*

Brynne returned from the concession stand, carrying a stack of cavity-causing snack foods. "What'd I miss?" She tottered through the row and sat on the other side of Lizette. Marnie cringed when she saw her lean over and whisper to Brynne, whose snide giggling grew louder and louder.

"Wow," Brynne said through a series of snickers. "That's *priceless.*"

Marnie's hands were going numb from gripping the armrest so hard. She wanted to tell Brynne off, but it was as if her tongue had been permanently relocated to Belgium or something.

Luckily Lizette was loosening up a bit. "Well, what does Nola have lined up?" she asked Marnie with interest.

Marnie looked skeptically at Lizette and Brynne. Was this some sort of trap? Were they just waiting for her to say something so they could whisper and laugh right in front of her? Regardless, she couldn't just sit there and stare at them like a zombie. "Um, I'm not sure. Maybe we'll play Scene It or something."

"Did you really just say, 'Scene It'?" Brynne was not trying very hard to hold back laughter.

"I like that game," Grier said sweetly.

Marnie gave Grier a look of appreciation and smiled. But that was where the happy vibes ended. This whole conversation was a disaster. Marnie could feel tears welling up in her eyes as she thought about how the girls might treat her tomorrow. Would they snub her? Or keep pulling this passive-aggressive stuff? She wasn't sure how much more of this she could take.

But then out of nowhere, Lizette came to Marnie's rescue. "The TV edition is my favorite."

Brynne immediately tried to save face. "Oh yeah, that one *is* good."

Lizette rolled her eyes and shifted in her seat so that her back was toward Brynne. "Listen, I have a better idea. Why don't you come over to my dad's summer place on Saturday night? It's right on Morgan Lake. He'll be closing it up next weekend for the season so it'll be our last chance to go until spring."

Marnie wasn't sure what to say. Lizette seemed to have changed her tune. Maybe she could salvage this episode from turning into a nightmare. "Well, um, it's very nice of you to offer —"

"The house is huge. And get this. My father had a book-release party a couple of weeks ago. It had a murder mystery theme and he still has all the costumes. We could, like, dress up and play a live-action version of 'Clue.'" Lizette was talking with so much enthusiasm that Marnie could feel her spirits lifting. Perhaps she wouldn't be shunned after all.

Grier bounced up and down in her seat. "That would be *so* much fun!"

Brynne summoned up enough energy to say, "I guess."

Marnie had to admit Lizette's idea was great. Much better than Scene It and most likely much better than anything she or Nola could cook up. She just had to make sure that Nola would be included — Marnie couldn't go through with this otherwise.

"I'll have to check with Nola," Marnie said warily. "But I'm sure she'll want to go just as much as I do."

Please, please *don't hate me,* she thought.

Brynne leaned in and whispered into Lizette's ear, but neither of them giggled afterward. Marnie held her breath, waiting for either one of them to kick her to the curb with their cork-soled heels.

Brynne handed Lizette a box of M&M's. She opened it up and offered some to Marnie before taking any herself. Marnie held out her hands as the candy spilled into her cupped palms.

"Well, let us know what she says." Lizette took all the blue ones out of Marnie's stash and popped them in her mouth one at a time. Then she smiled.

As the lights went down around them, Marnie heaved a sigh of relief — at least she would have a two-hour break from the stress. She was mentally exhausted. So much so that she fell asleep during the movie and didn't remember to turn her phone back on, even when she got home.

Chapter 15

"I have never seen this much lettuce in my life," Matt said as he rifled through the refrigerator. "Red leaf. Boston. Romaine. Wow."

He was searching for a can of Reddi-wip so that they could top off their hot chocolate with a thick spiral of whipped cream, but Nola had already warned him about her mom's health habits.

"I'll be surprised if you find anything sweet in there," Nola said as she poured hot water into two mugs filled with Swiss Miss. "I think the hot cocoa might have been left behind by the family who lived here before us."

Matt poked his head out from behind the door and smiled. "Well, if your mom doesn't believe in sugar, how do you explain the hyperactivity of the Terrible Twins?"

Nola walked over to the kitchen table and set their drinks down on two coasters. "Here's a theory. They come from a planet where all living organisms subsist solely on high-fructose corn syrup."

"That makes total sense." Matt shut the refrigerator door and sighed. "What doesn't make sense is that your family eats like herbivores, and that you don't have any Reddi-wip."

Nola studied Matt's shoulders when he sat down at the table with her. They seemed a lot broader now that he was wearing one of her father's T-shirts. Mr. James had been rail-thin when he met Mrs. James in college, and because his current diet consisted of whatever grew in their vegetable garden, his physique hadn't changed much since then. Matt, on the other hand, seemed to have a swimmer's body all of a sudden, and Nola was having a hard time ignoring all of its great features.

"Why is Reddi-wip so important?" Nola asked, hoping to take her mind off of how toned Matt's arms looked stirring his hot chocolate.

"Wow, you really have been brainwashed, haven't you?" When Matt licked his spoon, Nola thought her head might explode. "Okay, the reason is actually sentimental," he explained. "I used to be the neighborhood paperboy."

Nola smiled at the thought of it. "You? A *paperboy*?"

Matt acted offended. "What, don't I look like a young entrepreneur to you?"

"I'm sorry. Go on."

"Anyway, I used to get stuck in the rain all the time, and when I did, my mom would have hot chocolate with whipped cream waiting for me when I came home."

Nola had a hunch that her eyes were shining, so she looked down into her mug. "Aw, that's nice."

"Yeah, it was," she heard Matt say almost solemnly. She glanced up and saw a sad expression on Matt's face. She was about to ask him what was wrong when she heard bellowing voices from upstairs.

"Noooooo-laaaaaaaa!"

"Let us out of here!"

Nola and Matt broke into a fit of laughter.

"Do you think that locking them in their room without feeding them dinner was too harsh of a punishment?" she asked.

"No way. I especially liked the part when Dennis asked how long their time-out was for, and you said 'Infinity.'"

"What can I say? I'm brilliant."

Matt grinned and took a sip of his hot cocoa. "Cute and brilliant. A dangerous combo indeed."

Suddenly a familiar feeling came over Nola. Her skin was becoming warm and an itching sensation was spreading across her chest. She thought that drinking her entire cup of hot chocolate in one big gulp would help matters, but it didn't. There was no stopping it now.

All this because a boy called me cute! Nola thought. *I AM A FREAK GIRL!!!*

"Um, Nola," Matt said apprehensively. "Your skin is getting sort of blotchy."

"Is it?" Nola figured she might as well play it like this had never happened before. Why did Matt have to know she was a complete spaz? She peered down at her chest and pretended to be surprised. "Ew! Gross!"

"It's okay, I'm sure it's just hives or something. Are you allergic to chocolate?"

"I don't think so."

Matt seemed a bit perplexed, but then he snapped his fingers. "Oatmeal."

"Huh?"

"Are you itchy?" he asked.

Nola's skin felt as though it was covered in poison ivy, but she tried not to show it. "A little."

Matt got up and started rummaging around in the kitchen, opening up cupboards and checking out the pantry. "When I was six, I got chicken pox and my mom used to give me these oatmeal baths." He jumped up when he found what he was looking for — a large variety pack of oatmeal. "Look, up in the sky! It's a bird! It's a plane! It's Quakerman!"

"If you think I'm going to take a bath in breakfast cereal, you're crazy," Nola said, trying not to smile.

He took a step closer. "Don't you trust the Quakers? They founded Pennsylvania, you know."

Even though she was itchy all over, Nola couldn't

care less. She was laughing so hard. "I don't trust *you*. What if you're just making this up?"

When Matt closed in some more, Nola got up and pushed a chair in front of her for protection. "I'm not making it up," he said, chuckling.

"Yeah, well, I won't believe it until I talk to your mom," Nola said playfully.

The moment she said that, Matt's grin vanished and he stopped dead in his tracks. He set the box of oatmeal down on the table gently and shoved his hands in his pockets. It was very quiet until a loud series of beeps went off in the nearby laundry room.

"I guess my shirt is ready," he muttered.

Now Nola's stomach felt queasy. "I'll go get it."

She walked into the laundry room, which was down the hallway. She was so nervous her hands were shaking. What had happened out there? Had she said something wrong? Matt looked as though he'd been punched in the gut.

Nola opened up the dryer door and grabbed Matt's Green Day T-shirt. She brought it up to her nose and inhaled. It still smelled like Axe, but the aroma of autumn was definitely unmistakable. She closed her eyes for a second and remembered what Matt had looked like in the rain: his shaggy hair falling into his face, the way the raindrops streaked down his cheeks and pointy chin, how his crooked smile was like a ray of sunshine in the storm.

She wanted to hide in the laundry room forever, thinking thoughts like these, but she had to face whatever weirdness was lurking around the corner. Nola took a deep breath and returned to the kitchen. However, she nearly fainted when she saw Matt shirtless, holding her dad's shirt in his hands.

Whooooooooooooa.

Nola never thought of Matt as the hot type. Cute, maybe. Quirky, definitely. But hot? Not exactly.

All that changed instantly. Matt was totally ripped — not in a steroid-happy bodybuilder kind of way, but in a flat stomach, Olympic-gold-medalist swimmer kind of way. How did a physics geek/bass player like him get this buff?

"So what's Mirapex?" he asked.

She had to shake her head a bit in order to come back to reality. "Oh, it's a drug that treats Parkinson's disease."

Matt held up the shirt and read the writing on the back. "And who's Boehringer Ingelheim?"

Nola's mouth nearly fell open when she saw his ab muscles contract. "Um . . . it's the pharmaceutical company my dad works for. He's a sales rep."

Matt nodded and tossed it onto the back of a kitchen

chair. Nola handed him his shirt and gave him a friendly smile.

"Nice and warm," she said.

Matt slipped it on and smiled back. "Thanks."

There was an awkward pause. Nola kept thinking about what happened a few minutes ago and wished she knew what to do.

"Well, I should head home," Matt said. "It's getting late."

Nola wrung her hands. "Okay. Thanks for dropping off my book."

"Thanks for the dry T-shirt," he said, grinning again.

"Thanks for the ideas for Marnie's party," she replied.

"I stand by my jousting suggestion. If the people at Medieval Times can do it, why can't you?"

She walked Matt out the front door and stood on the porch, where she watched him put on his messenger bag and get on his bike. She was about to wave good-bye when Matt glanced up and gave her a smile so genuine she almost collapsed.

There is just no way Matt could have gotten suspended from school, Nola thought. It just wasn't in him. Lizette had to be lying.

"Thanks for finally relaxing and being yourself," he

said with a wink. Then he pedaled off in the direction of the moonlight that was streaking through the sky.

When Nola strolled back into the house, she went to the bathroom so she could put some calamine lotion on her hives.

But they were miraculously gone.

Wednesday, Sept 12, 6:45 P.M.

nolaj1994: *hi there*
marniebird: *HEY! how r u?*
nolaj1994: *ok. where've u been?*
marniebird: *i know, i've been totally MIA lately. soooooo sorry*
nolaj1994: *did u get my messages?*
marniebird: *yes, just been busy. so lady . . . MATT WAS OVER???*
nolaj1994: *here we go*
marniebird: *tell me everything!*
nolaj1994: *he just stopped by to give me my physics workbook*
marniebird: *u mean he stopped by so he could flirt with you!*
nolaj1994: *NO!*
marniebird: *hahahahahaha. jk, nol.*
nolaj1994: *well, he did take his shirt off*
marniebird: *HE DID?*
nolaj1994: *pip and squeak locked us out in the rain, so i loaned him one of Dad's shirts. anyway, when his was dry, he took off the other shirt, blah blah blah*
marniebird: *wow. was he hot?*
nolaj1994: *so hot my retinas burned off*
marniebird: *LOL. did u ask him about being suspended?*

nolaj1994: *no, why would i?*

marniebird: *dunno. just thought u would b curious*

nolaj1994: *well i'm not cuz i know it's not true*

marniebird: *maybe it is though*

nolaj1994: *doubt it*

marniebird: *there's only 1 way to find out*

nolaj1994: *i suppose. he did come up with some awesome party ideas though. can't wait to run them by u!*

marniebird: *oh, there's something i need to tell u about the party*

nolaj1994: *what?*

marniebird: *well LL, brynne, and grier said they'd come*

nolaj1994: *all right. i'll get extra supplies then*

marniebird: *that's so nice of you!*

nolaj1994: *np*

marniebird: *but there's 1 more thing. and i hope ur not mad because u know how much i ♥ u and am so grateful for all ur planning. but LL's dad has a place up on morgan lake and it's the last weekend the house is going to be open, so she thought it might be fun to throw the party there. and you know, her dad has these leftover costumes from his latest book party, and we can use them, too, and have this like murder mystery theme and everything. anyway, i just thought it would b nice 2 do something different. u upset?*

nolaj1994 is idle at 7:05 P.M.

marniebird: *???????????*

nolaj1994 is no longer idle at 8:33 P.M.

nolaj1994: *hi*

marniebird: *where did u go?*

nolaj1994: *sorry my mom brought home KFC, the boys went berserk, she must have gone temporarily insane*

marniebird: *i called & texted but ur phone was off*

nolaj1994: *just been busy, u know how it is*

marniebird: *c'mon, don't be like that*

nolaj1994: *i'm not being like anything*

marniebird: *if ur mad, just say ur mad*

nolaj1994: *i'm not mad, i'm confused. when did all of this get decided?*

marniebird: *yesterday*

nolaj1994: *but i texted a bunch of times about the party, why didn't u mention it then?*

marniebird: *we were at the movies, and then i forgot to turn my phone back on when i left. if it's a big deal, nol, i'll tell LL that we're having it at my house. seriously, i don't want u 2 b upset*

nolaj1994: *but u'd rather do the murder mystery thing, right?*

marniebird: *well, i think it sounds fun. dressing up in these fancy period costumes and being near the lake. don't u think it sounds cool?*

nolaj1994: *honestly, i think it's really silly. but it's ur birthday, marn. if this is what u want to do, then that's what we'll do*

marniebird: *u sure?*

nolaj1994: *yes*

marniebird: *THANK U THANK U THANK U. i'll make it up to u, promise*

nolaj1994: *u and ur promises*

marniebird: *the party is going 2 b amazing*

nolaj1994: *if u say so*

marniebird: *i know so ☺. ok, have 2 do homework*

nolaj1994: *me 2*

marniebird: *LYLAS*

nolaj1994: *LYLAS*

Chapter 16

At 3:01 P.M. on Thursday, Marnie was wearing a safari-inspired shirtdress from Forever 21 and sitting in lecture hall 4 with a large group of kids who wanted to become cogs in the well-oiled democracy machine at Poughkeepsie Central High School. She had even bigger aspirations, though, like making Dane Harris fall madly in love with her. She glanced down at the list she'd started.

WAYS I CAN GET DANE TO NOTICE ME

1) Attend every student council meeting . . . wearing fishnets. Yeow!
2) Put my hair up more often and show off my long neck.
3) Use more John Frieda Sheer Blonde products. Erin always says boys love blondes!
4) Drop something on the floor in front of him so I'll have to bend over and pick it up. This is in every teen movie and it always works. Worth a try.
5) Research the competition.

Marnie looked up and checked out some of the upperclassmen in the room. Unfortunately the competition was stiff. For instance, there were two *very* cool Majors nearby — juniors Keri-Anne Willman (cutie-pie daughter of Poughkeepsie's most notorious lawyer) and Deirdre Boyd (Delia's catalog model and infamous field hockey striker). Erin Fitzpatrick had passed the popularity torch to them when she graduated a few months ago, and they were truly doing Marnie's big sister proud. Every person within a few feet of Keri-Anne and Deirdre was either staring at them adoringly, laughing at something they had said, or offering up their internal organs if either of them ever needed one in an emergency.

Marnie could feel her insecurities preparing for liftoff. She'd heard from Lizette how Dane was worshipped by all, but primarily ran with the oh-so-fabulous Majors, which in most cases were juniors and seniors. How was she going to ever find a way to stand out in that ultra in-crowd? She couldn't ride on Erin's coattails forever, that was for sure.

But then the door was flung open, and immediately Marnie relaxed. Everything was going to be okay now, for there she was, her savior: Lizette Levin, decked out in a flowing white prairie shirt, cowboy boots, and a pair of pajama bottoms with tiny purple cupcakes dotted all over the thin, almost-sheer fabric.

Lizette sashayed through the room like she owned it and parked herself right next to ... Keri-Anne and Deirdre.

So much for relaxing.

Marnie's shoulders tensed up the second she saw Lizette lean in and whisper to the both of them. Life ran in slow motion after that. *Keri-Anne ... threw ... her ... head ... back ... and ... guffawed. Deirdre ... put ... her ... hand ... over ... her ... mouth ... to ... quiet ... her ... witchlike ... cackle.* Then Marnie heard her own name in her ear and things were back to normal speed. Only for a second, though.

Holy cannoli.

Dane. Harris. Is. Sitting. Right. Next. To. Me.

"I had a feeling you were a Leek," he said, leaning back in his chair and extending his long legs out into the aisle.

Marnie took in the sight of him and nearly lost consciousness. How could Lizette think he was *dull?* Sure, he dressed as though he had a khaki pants factory in his basement and a personal maid to iron his J. Crew button-down shirts. Other than that, though, he was the personification of intriguing: witty, smart, nice, flirty, and *so gorgeous* that Madame Tussaud's had probably offered his parents big money to create a wax figure of his likeness. The cheekbones, the sparkling blue eyes, the not-a-strand-out-of-place hair, the tall, lean Luke Wilson–type body — all of it needed to be preserved so that future generations could appreciate his beauty!

"What makes you think I'm a leadership geek?" Marnie asked, crossing her arms in front of her chest.

Dane didn't even bother to avert his eyes. "I have my reasons."

"And they are?"

Dane leaned forward and pushed his desk to the left so he was a little closer to Marnie. "It's a secret."

Marnie's pulse quickened. From this proximity, she could see just how perfectly symmetrical Dane's face was. And despite the party-boy rumors, Dane seemed like a stand-up guy. One thing was for sure: There was no way Dane could ever hurt like Weston had. "You can tell me, can't you?" Marnie asked.

Dane was about to answer when the door flew open once again, startling everyone. In walked a short boy with dark square-rimmed glasses who could pass for Jamie Lynn Spears's dorky friend Chase on *Zoey 101*. He was carrying a stack of thick packets and seemed quite panic-stricken.

"Oh no," Dane muttered. "Jeremy Atwood."

Marnie watched as the boy began weaving in and out of the desks, distributing the books with intensity. One landed on her desk with a loud *thud*, and then he was on to the next person. "I think he's in my homeroom."

Dane stood and rolled up his sleeves as if he was about to get his hands dirty. "Will you excuse me for a minute?"

Look at the manners on this guy!

"Sure," she replied with a smile.

Dane grinned back. "Don't go anywhere, okay?"

Marnie's face was getting hot. "I won't."

He walked toward the front of the room and cleared his throat. "Hey, everybody. Thanks for coming."

The group quieted down and turned their attention to Dane.

"What Jeremy passed out is the student government handbook," Dane continued with a smile, "which is basically a code of ethics that all members need to follow. But before we go over that, I'd like to get nominations for freshman class officers out of the way." Dane was so good at public speaking that he didn't trip over a single word. Marnie was amazed.

When Dane began explaining the nominations process, she quickly glanced over her shoulder. For a moment, she swore that she saw Lizette huddled together with Deirdre and Keri-Anne. But she turned her head the moment Lizette pointed in Marnie's direction, and Deirdre and Keri-Anne started to stare at her.

Oh no, are they talking about me? Marnie thought.

"So let's start off with the lower positions first. Remember, you can only nominate someone from your own class, including yourself. And someone else has to second your nomination," Dane said, making careful eye contact with each person. "All right, I'm opening the floor for nominations for freshman class treasurer."

"I would like to nominate Jeremy Atwood," a voice boomed from the back row.

Marnie turned around to see who'd spoken. Lo and behold, it was Jeremy himself. Every student in the room started chuckling until Dane clapped his hands together once and restored order.

"Do I have any seconds?" Dane asked the group.

Marnie looked around and saw that no one was taking the bait. Apparently nobody thought this high-strung, odd, quirky guy was very worthy of the title. But Marnie could tell from the enthusiastic smile on his face that he really wanted this position. So what was the harm of giving him a chance? If Nola were around, she'd agree with her 100 percent.

Marnie raised her hand. "I second the nomination."

"Um, thanks," Dane said, looking confused.

When Marnie heard the snickers coming from Lizette's

little trio, she slowly lowered her hand and slid down in her seat. She was obviously getting on Lizette's bad side.

"Does anyone else have a nomination for freshman class treasurer?" Dane asked.

"I'd like to nominate Marnie Fitzpatrick."

Marnie whipped her head around and saw Lizette with her hand raised.

What is she doing?

Marnie didn't mind being in student government per se, but being responsible for all sorts of treasure-y things was definitely *not* something she wanted.

A gasp came from the back of the room, and Marnie saw Jeremy standing up, waving his arms frantically.

Dane pointed at him. "Yes, Jeremy?"

"Is that legal? Marnie already seconded my nomination," Jeremy asked breathlessly.

"Actually, it is," Dane answered. Jeremy sat back down and scowled. "Anyone second the nomination?"

Marnie closed her eyes and chanted in her hand: *no, no, no, no, no, no, no.*

"I'd like to second," said a light-and-bubbly voice from the front row.

Marnie opened her eyes and saw that it had come from a girl with an unforgettable mop of curly hair.

That Sally Applebaum and her stupid diplomat complex!

"Good." From the size of Dane's grin, it seemed as

though he was pleased with this turn of events. "Are there any more?"

"I'd like to request a recount!" Jeremy shouted at the top of his lungs. Marnie guessed he had really hoped to run unopposed.

Dane rolled his eyes. "There's no point in recounting *two* votes, man."

Jeremy bolted up again, as if to emphasize his outrage. "But she's not serious about this. I mean, her kind treats student council as though it's some sort of *sorority* or something."

Marnie's eyes widened with shock. Her *kind*? He didn't even *know* her! And to think that she seconded his silly self-nomination out of sympathy! She was about to raise her hand, but someone else had already beat her to it.

"Um, *Jeremy*, just because you're afraid that Marnie will beat you hands-down in this election doesn't mean that you can insult her in front of everyone." Lizette was standing, hands on her hips.

Marnie's heart skipped ten beats. Lizette was actually sticking up for her! As for Jeremy, he huffed loudly and flopped back down in his seat without another word.

Everyone began filing out of the room when the meeting was over, and the rest of the candidates were chosen, including two more nominees for freshman class treasurer. Dane was the first to leave, so Marnie took her time gathering her things together. Her L.L. Bean tote bag was filled to the brim with books, so when she slung it over her shoulder she nearly knocked herself over. Then she felt an elbow nudge her in the side.

"Jeremy is a *loser*," Lizette said, pulling a piece of lint off of Marnie's dress. "Don't even sweat it."

"Lizette, why did you nominate me?" Marnie made sure that she didn't sound annoyed or anything.

"Well, I was talking to Deirdre and Keri-Anne. They're sick of certain underclassmen wrecking the student council. They said they wanted someone cool for a change, so I told them about you." Lizette reached into her pajama pants pocket and brought out a pack of spearmint Orbit. "Want some?"

Marnie was overjoyed. Lizette Levin — the authority on coolness — thought *she* was cool! Not only that, but she'd done something that Nola would never have done. She'd gotten up in front of a room full of people and told off Jeremy Atwood. Not that Marnie was trying to compare the two of them, but how could she avoid it?

Lizette was the anti-Nola: bold, daring, trendy, and fearless. Of course, that didn't mean Marnie couldn't be friends with both of them. It didn't even mean that Nola and Lizette would never become friends, either. It just meant that Marnie was glad Lizette was around today, instead of Nola.

"So how do you know Deirdre and Keri-Anne, anyway?" Marnie took a piece of gum and walked out of the classroom with Lizette.

"They're in my Asana class at Arlington Yoga Works." She did a quick tree pose and smiled.

"You're kidding."

"No, I'm not." Lizette blew a big bubble and broke it with her ring finger. Then she started laughing. "Last week Deirdre fell on her head while trying to do the Crow. Don't tell anyone though, 'cuz she'll kill me!"

Marnie started giggling, too. "I won't tell."

"Good." Lizette looked down at her huge cuff watch. "Ugh, I'm late. My dad's going to flip out. Hey, do you want to come decorate the lake house with me tonight?"

Marnie winced. She'd told Nola that she'd stop by after the meeting was over and make a batch of organic Rice Krispie treats. "Um . . . well —"

"You can bring Nola if you want," Lizette cut her off. "I don't care."

Marnie studied Lizette's face to see if she was being sincere. "Are you sure?"

"Yeah, whatever," she said. "I'm going to run out to the car, so hurry up."

"Okay, I'll give her a call."

Marnie fished out her phone from her crowded tote bag as she listened to Lizette clomp down the hall. She speed-dialed Nola's number and anxiously waited for Nola to pick up.

"Hey, Marn," she answered. "How was the meeting? Did Dane ask you to be his first lady or what?"

"It was crazy, actually," Marnie said. "But never mind that now. Lizette just asked us if we could help her decorate the lake house for my party. Isn't that awesome?"

There was a pause — a really long pause.

"But you were supposed to come over," Nola said.

Marnie took the phone away from her ear so she could see the time. She didn't want to keep Lizette waiting. "I know, but she just asked me when we left the meeting."

There was an even longer pause.

She heard Nola clear her throat. "Yeah, well, I've already made a mess in the kitchen and put out all the stuff for the treats."

"Can't you just put it back?" Marnie said, annoyed.

"I guess," Nola mumbled.

Marnie ran her free hand through her hair. Why did Nola always have to be so difficult? "If you don't want to go, just say so."

She heard Nola sigh. "Sorry, I just thought we were going to spend time together."

"If you come with me, we *will* be spending time together," Marnie pointed out, trying to gently coax her.

Nola sighed again, but this time Marnie could tell it was out of frustration. "That's not what I meant."

Marnie heard her phone beep. "Hold on a sec." She checked her cell and saw there was a text message in her in-box.

R U COMING OR NOT?

Lizette.

Argh!!!

"Nola, I —"

"Just go ahead without me," she interrupted. "I have tons of other stuff to do anyway."

Marnie knew her best friend well enough to know that she was lying. "Come on, Nol."

"Really, go decorate your brains out. We have our Friday sleepover tomorrow anyway," she replied. "Maybe I'll swing by Hoe Bowl and watch the pros. Our next Saturday night battle is in two weeks."

Marnie started jogging toward the entrance to the school, but her bag was weighing her down. "That's right." It was as if she had tunnel vision, and the only thing she could see was the front door, and the only thing she could hear was the idling engine of Mr. Levin's luxury SUV.

"Have fun," Nola said. "Call me later, okay?"

"Sure," Marnie said before hanging up the phone, and before she could make any promises.

Chapter 17

After a grilled-tofu-in-sweet-chili-sauce dinner, Nola sat cross-legged on the living room window seat, surrounded by jewelry-making supplies. Her father had taken the boys out to Stewart's for Italian ices a few minutes ago. He'd asked Nola if she wanted to come along — he even offered to share some sorbet with her — but she didn't want to give up the precious opportunity to work on Marnie's bracelet without having a Nerf football whiz by her head.

She had lined up all of the beads she wanted to use and gotten the appropriate tools out of the drawers. Now she just had to link the beads together on this piece of elastic. Nola had made Marnie jewelry before — there was the silver pendant with the jade stone she'd given her when they'd graduated from eighth grade, and the ring she'd woven out of her mom's leftover yarn — but this bracelet was special, and not just because of the occasion.

Two years ago, Nola and Marnie had gone on a weekend-long class trip to New York City. They had ridden on one of those red "hop-on, hop-off" double-decker sightseeing buses that go to the Metropolitan Museum of Art, the Empire State Building, Times Square, and all the usual tourist destinations. Surprisingly, Nola's favorite stop was SoHo, where Marnie and one of their chaperones, Mrs. Schubert, lost themselves in designer boutiques for hours. Nola fell in love with the vendors who had set up tables on and around Prince Street. Each merchant was selling something beautiful and hand-made — scarves, blankets, rugs, clothes, lampshades, and more. But what really caught her eye was the hand-crafted jewelry. The silver chains and hammered gold bracelets had glinted in the late spring sun. The dark onyx and pale jade stones had been smooth to the touch.

When Nola saw a particular bracelet lying on a black-felt-covered folding table, she stopped cold. It was made out of an assortment of brightly colored glass beads and small pieces of oddly shaped stones. She spent the last of her money on it and had wanted to give it to Marnie as a gift, but she'd accidentally left it on the bus back to the hotel. She was devastated, of course. But that bracelet was what had inspired her to start making her own jewelry, so she looked back on the memory with fondness.

Now Nola wanted to make this bracelet as incredi-ble as that one from SoHo. She knew for sure that Marnie was going to love it. But these days, Nola felt as though this was the only thing she knew for sure.

Marnie hadn't been acting like herself at all, and Nola was kind of hurt that she was expected to roll with whatever Marnie wanted, no questions asked.

As Nola picked up each bead and inspected it for nicks or imperfections, she wondered when Marnie had become so concerned with doing everything differently. What was wrong with what they had up until now? Nola was more than happy carrying on and letting things be, and not because she was scared to change. Okay, that was part of it, but still, Nola liked their friendship as it was. She liked her life as it was. She liked planning her best friend's birthday party, which she'd done ever since Mrs. Fitzpatrick handed over the duties three years ago. Now Marnie had given that responsibility to someone she barely even knew, and Nola couldn't understand why.

Nola set the beads down and wiped at her eyes. *Do not cry. Do. Not. Cry,* she told herself. But it was no use. Usually when things like this happened, she'd pick up the phone and call the only person who truly knew her, but that person was now out at someone else's house when she was supposed to be here. Not only that, that person *was* the reason Nola was sad. Who would she turn to now?

She bent over and picked up her cell, which she'd placed on the floor, just in case Marnie called. Nola thought about getting in touch with her mom at the hospital. It was 7:30 P.M. She'd be on break and would have some time to talk. Nola dialed half of the number (her mom had made her memorize it so that if she ever lost her phone in a crisis, she'd know what number to call), but then hit the END button. Her mom had enough drama going on in the ER. The last thing she'd want to do on her break was talk her daughter down off an emotional ledge.

Nola closed her eyes and tried not to shed any more tears. She tried to think of what her mom would say if she were there. More often than not, her mom's inspiring anecdotes included sayings like, "When the going gets tough, the tough . . . make a casserole!" (Nola had recently discovered that her mom's words of wisdom came right out of *Ladies' Home Journal*.)

She was startled when her phone went off right in her hand. After catching her breath, she looked at the caller ID.

MATT H.

Nola smiled as she remembered exchanging numbers with him during physics class. She cleared her throat before picking up. "Hello?"

Matt's voice was energetic and breezy on the other end. "Hi, Nola. What's up?"

She got up off the window seat and began pacing

around nervously. "Nothing much. I'm just in the middle of some arts and crafts."

"Ooooh, crafts. Tell me more."

Nola covered her mouth with her hand as if Matt was in the room with her and could actually see her grinning from ear to ear. "I'm making a bracelet for Marnie. It's her birthday on Saturday."

"Right. I remember the paper-clip necklace you wore on the first day of school. That was awesome."

Nola's head was buzzing with excitement. *He thought my necklace was awesome!*

"Well, this one has a higher degree of difficulty," she replied, trying to sound casual.

"Are you making this bracelet out of staples or something?"

Nola laughed. "No, I didn't have time to run to OfficeMax."

"Bummer." She could hear Matt plucking at his bass guitar, the strings reverberating with this low, deep tone. "I can't wait to see what you create though."

"Really?"

"Yeah, I dig art. And the artists who make it."

Wait, is he trying to say he likes me? Nola could swear that Matt had used some sort of line.

But then Nola heard a girl laughing, and there was no one in her house but her.

"No, it's B, then G," Matt said.

Nola shook her head in confusion. "What?"

"Nothing." A few more notes echoed from his bass. "So, uh, is Marnie having a party?"

"Um, yeah. Just a small one though," Nola explained while trying to ignore what she thought she'd heard. "It'll be me, Marnie, and a few other people."

"Cool," Matt said, sounding distracted. There was a series of muffled laughs in the background, definitely from a girl and definitely coming from Matt's phone. "You have to press down harder, like this."

Nola's eyes grew wide. What was going on over there? "Are you . . . *busy?*"

"I'm multi-tasking," Matt said, and then chuckled. "Hold on a sec." His voice sounded fainter now, like he'd pulled the phone away from his mouth. "Why don't you take five, okay? Go get a drink in the kitchen. Oh, and bring me back a Sprite!"

Nola grabbed at her stomach. She couldn't believe this, but she was nauseous at the thought of another girl being with Matt! This was bad news. Bad news to the millionth power.

He came back to the phone out of breath. "Sorry. I was just giving someone a lesson."

Her stomach cramped again. *A "lesson"?* she wanted to demand. *Who is "someone"?*

A crashing sound nearly shattered Nola's eardrum. "Ow!" Matt shouted.

"You okay?"

"Nola, you are my witness. I will never volunteer my services again. The acoustics in my room have been tainted."

"That bad, huh?"

"I should have followed my instincts," he said through a loud commotion that sounded like guitars being dropped from the top of a skyscraper. "This person has no musical talent whatsoever. I don't think she could even play the tambourine, because that would mean she'd have to find her rhythm, which is most likely buried under a rock. Actually, make that a boulder."

Nola's heart sank. A girl was in Matt's room. A girl was sitting close enough to him so that he could give her *lessons*. A GIRL.

"Do you want me to call you back?" Nola asked. She really wanted to get off the phone before the girl came back with Matt's Sprite, possibly wearing nothing but a guitar pick.

"No way," he said. "Trust me, she and I are done. Besides, I'd rather be talking to you."

Nola grinned and flopped down on the sofa, her stomach a little less tense. Maybe she was overreacting. Still, even though Matt's comment seemed heartfelt, she wanted to make sure he wasn't just kidding with her. "Well, you don't want to be rude to your hot date, do you?"

She heard what sounded like a door squeak open, and then Matt started laughing hysterically. "Hey, Iris, check it out. Nola thinks that you and I are on a hot date!"

Nola slapped her forehead. *I am so busted!*

"Girlfriend, do you think I'd disrespect myself by going out with this loser?" Iris had obviously snatched the phone away from Matt.

"I was only joking," Nola murmured.

"Don't tell *anyone* I was over here!" Iris snapped before handing the phone over.

"She just doesn't want a certain someone to find out that she's taking bass lessons to impress him," Matt teased.

Nola giggled when she heard Iris scream, "I hate you!" followed by a swatting sound, Matt yelping, and the slam of a door.

"She's mad," he said. "So I better not tell you who the certain someone is."

"Like you said before, you should follow your instincts." Nola lay down and put her bare feet up on the arm of the couch. Her legs were itchy, so she pulled up her gray yoga pants to her knees and checked for hives. She sighed in relief when all she saw was a patch of dry skin.

"So now that it's just you and me, what should we talk about?" he asked.

Nola pictured him lying on his bed and looking up at the ceiling, which she always did when she talked on the phone with Marnie. "Your room. What does it look like?"

Matt laughed. "It's a mess. Dirty clothes on one side, clean clothes are . . . somewhere around here. Let's see. Uh, on one of my walls I've got a poster of glam-rock-era David Bowie. It was a present from my dad, so I had to put it up, but I'd rather have something else."

"Like what?"

"Jessica Alba in a string bikini, hands down!"

"I thought you were going to name some sort of bass wizard, like Flea from Red Hot Chili Peppers," Nola said, snickering.

"Nice one," Matt said, sounding impressed. "Are you into music?"

"Yeah, all kinds." Nola tried to think of every mp3 file on her iPod. She wondered what bands she and Matt had in common and if they shared some of the same songs on their playlists.

But two hours later, she didn't have to wonder much about Matt anymore. They had covered practically every topic in the universe — favorite pop groups that they'd never admit to liking (Nola was a secret Pussycat Dolls fan, and Matt said he owned a few Avril Lavigne albums), food they could eat every day of their life (Matt said Cinnamon Toast Crunch cereal and meatball subs from Jelly Belly Deli were tied, while Nola voted for her grandmother's homemade beef stew, which she hadn't been allowed to eat in years), and if they could travel to any place, where would they go (Nola had trouble deciding between Greece and Italy, while Matt's was a no-brainer: Amsterdam).

Nola had moved up to her room when her father and brothers returned from Stewart's. She'd locked her door and spent the rest of the time talking to Matt spread out on her bed, legs dangling off to the side. She didn't even notice that the evening sky had gone pitch-black, and she hadn't even turned the light on. She couldn't remember being so engrossed in a conversation that she lost track of everything that was going on around her. There wasn't even the slightest bit of the weirdness they'd experienced the other night. It was amazing.

"Okay, now that I've told you everything that's in

my room and then some," Matt said, still slapping away at his bass, "when are you going to come over and see it for yourself?"

Nola shot up out of bed. *He really is asking me out this time! What should I do? I've got to talk to Marnie.*

She sprinted across the room to her desk, shook the mouse, and woke up her PC. The light from the monitor filled the room as she called up her IM list to see if Marnie was online. She had to be home by now. How long did decorating a lake house take?

"Um . . . I don't know. Soon." Nola's heart was pounding so hard, she wouldn't have been surprised if Matt could hear it over the phone.

marniebird is currently online.

Whew!
"Well, what about tomorrow?" he said.

But Nola was only half listening. She was too busy typing as fast as she could.

nolaj1994: *HELP! MATT IS ASKING ME OUT!*

Nola waited a few seconds before frantically writing something again. In the meantime, she tried to stall with Matt. "Tomorrow? Um . . . let me check my Out-look calendar."

He laughed. "Outlook calendar? Wow, you must be in demand."

nolaj1994: *marnie? r u there? I need u!*

Nothing. Nola checked Marnie's status once more. It didn't say that she was idle. Why wasn't she answering?

"Um, yeah, there's all that . . . stuff I've got to do," she said absentmindedly.

"Right," he said.

"And Marnie's staying over tomorrow night."

"How's Sunday, then?"

Nola stared at the monitor, willing her IM window to receive a message from Marnie. But as seconds ticked away, all Nola saw was the flicking of her cursor over the words *I need u.*

"Sunday is good." She tried to sound upbeat, but her voice came out as soft as a whisper.

"Great," he said. "Maybe I can teach you how to play bass, and you can teach me how to make a belt out of rubber bands."

Nola laughed, but not as hard as she usually did when Matt said something funny. She couldn't take her eyes off the IM window.

"See ya later," he said happily.

Nola typed something on her computer and shut it down as she told him, "Good-bye."

nolaj1994: *just forget it*

nolaj1994 ʌigned off at 9:35 P.M.

Chapter 18

PRE-PARTY ERRANDS

1) Order small bottle of Philosophy Amazing Grace perfume from Sephora.com.

2) Search Erin's room for the eyelash curler she borrowed and claimed to have left behind — who does she think she's kidding? She always loses my stuff!

3) Call Uncle Zach and Aunt Sheila to thank them for their early b-day gift (*Chicken Soup for the Teenage Soul* — so cheesy, but secretly I love it).

4) Make sure Nola brings *Scene It*, just in case the party gets boring. (This is highly unlikely, though — Lizette is a party pro.)

When Marnie got back from her Friday-morning jog, all she wanted to do was collapse on her bed and go back to sleep. Decorating Lizette's lake house had been no easy task. The place was gigantic, and Lizette was a bit OCD when it came to "setting the scene," as she put it.

But getting more rest was out of the question. Marnie's mom had called her into the kitchen for a maple-and-brown-sugar oatmeal breakfast. The scent of it was one of her favorite things, mainly because it reminded Marnie of breakfasts with her father. They had loved that oatmeal equally and would often spend Saturday mornings devouring big bowls of it while watching cartoons. Marnie hadn't heard from her father in a while. She hoped that she'd get a call on her birthday, but the way things were going between him and her mom, she had a feeling that he was probably going to lie low.

Marnie tried to put negative thoughts out of her head as she washed her hands and sat down in front of a heaping bowl of warm oat goodness. "Mmmm . . . this looks delicious. Thanks, Mom."

"You're welcome." Her mother peeled off her apron and rooster-shaped oven mitt, and took a seat at the dark birch wood table. It was a family heirloom, and Mrs. Fitzpatrick always insisted that meals should be eaten there, which is why she'd nearly mud-wrestled her ex-husband in order to keep it. "So, how was your run?"

Marnie licked her lips after she slurped her first spoonful. "It was good."

"Erin called last night while you were out. She said she was sorry that she was going to miss your birthday," her mom said. "She's studying for a big test."

"Yeah, right," Marnie muttered.

"I just hope she doesn't strain herself and neglect her social life. College is supposed to be fun," her mom added.

"Oh, Mom, if Erin forgets to be popular, I'm sure you'll remind her." The sarcasm in Marnie's voice was undeniable.

"Don't be a grouch." Her mom pushed herself away from the table, went to the fridge, and poured a glass of orange juice.

Marnie rolled her eyes. She was surprised her mom hadn't changed her name to Susan Eleanor McBitter-pants when she got divorced.

"Speaking of your birthday, you never told me what you and Nola will be up to," her mom said.

Marnie picked up the pace with her spoon. She didn't want to get into too many details about Lizette and the party and set off her mom's highly sensitive buzz-kill alarm. "The usual."

"Really?" A puzzled expression appeared on her mom's face.

"What?"

"Nothing, I just thought that . . . never mind."

Marnie set her spoon down and stared at her mom. "Never mind, what?"

Her mom took a few gulps of orange juice. It was

obvious she was stalling. "You know I love Nola. She's like a daughter to me, and she's the sweetest little thing in the world."

Marnie furrowed her brow. She had no idea where her mom was going with this.

"I just thought that now that you're in high school, you'd . . . you know . . . branch out, make lots of new friends, like Erin did," she said.

Suddenly Marnie's stomach was churning. As if she wasn't under enough stress already! She didn't have to be a genius to figure out her mom wanted her to be more like Erin, but to actually hear the words coming from her mother's mouth was just too much to bear. "What are you trying to say, Mom? That there's something wrong with Nola? Or that there's something wrong with *me* because I haven't achieved class-A status like Erin?"

Her mom spilled the rest of her juice down the sink and set the glass down on the counter with extra force. "You're putting words in my mouth, Marnie."

"Am I?" She could feel her muscles tying into one big knot. "Why don't you explain what you mean then?"

Her mom returned to the table, sat down, and reached for Marnie's hand, but Marnie pulled away. "Nothing's wrong with you or with Nola. You guys have a close friendship, and that's so hard to find."

Marnie could feel tears welling up in her eyes. It was true. Their friendship was one of those sisterly, Hilary and Haylie Duff-type of friendships, but she knew deep down that things were changing, more than she had ever imagined they would.

"But you've always looked after Nola, kind of like the sister she never had," her mom went on. "And I've just been worried that, well, it's a big responsibility to be the center of someone's universe, isn't it?"

"I guess," Marnie said gruffly. That one drawback of being Nola's friend was hardly the point. Lately her loyalties were being divided and it was making her life complicated. Just the thought of possibly having to choose between Lizette and Nola was making her teary-eyed. "I'm just . . . scared," she whispered.

"Of what?" her mom asked.

Marnie searched herself and found her deepest fear, the thing she could never tell Nola, even if she wanted to. "There's this girl — Lizette. She's really popular, like the Erin kind of popular. Well, last night I was at *her* house, not Nola's." She paused and looked at her mom for a reaction, but she was just sitting patiently, waiting to hear more. "She wants to have my party there and . . ." Marnie's voice began to crack. "I'm afraid that she won't like Nola, and . . . then she won't like *me* anymore."

Marnie felt awful for saying this, so awful she started

sobbing. How could she be more worried about what Lizette thought than Nola's feelings?

Her mom wrapped her arms around Marnie and held her tight. "It's okay to be scared, but you know what? Lizette could like both of you, or neither of you, or just one of you. It's not the end of the world."

"Ugh, Mom, I *know!*" Marnie said sharply, worming away from her mother. She wiped at her eyes with her hands.

"So then stop acting like it is!" her mom snapped back. Apparently she was not in the mood for any of her daughter's attitude.

Marnie shot up from the table. "Fine, I won't!"

She stomped off into the living room and sat down in front of the computer, hoping that reviewing her party-errands list would help distract her from everything. (Mr. Fitzpatrick had seen a two-hour *Dateline* special on teens getting stalked by creeps over the Internet, so neither Erin nor Marnie had been allowed to have a computer in their bedrooms.) Marnie turned on the PC and waited for it to boot up, which seemed to take an eternity. Finally the desktop flashed on the screen. Marnie was about to open Microsoft Word when a pop-up window appeared:

You have three missed instant messages.

Marnie's brow furrowed as she clicked on the first message.

nolaj1994: *HELP! MATT IS ASKING ME OUT!*
Sent Thursday, September 13 at 9:31 P.M.

She swallowed hard when she clicked on the next one.

nolaj1994: *marnie? r u there? I need u!*
Sent Thursday, September 13 at 9:33 P.M.

Oh, no.

nolaj1994: *just forget it*
Sent Thursday, September 13 at 9:34 P.M.

How could this have happened? Marnie had been online for a couple of minutes before she went to bed last night. She thought she had logged off, but maybe she hadn't and Nola had assumed that she was still on and ignoring her.

"Hey, Mom," Marnie called out anxiously. "Did I forget to shut down the computer yesterday?"

"Yes, you did. I wish you'd be more careful about

that, Marnie. The last thing I need are my energy bills going through the roof," she replied.

Great!

Marnie brought up her Buddy List and saw that Nola was online. She began typing frantically.

marniebird: *nol, i didn't blow u off last night! u gotta believe me!*

After a few seconds passed, Nola wrote back.

nolaj1994: *whatev*

Oh no, Marnie thought. *She's mad.*

marniebird: *meet me B4 school on the front steps and i'll explain*

This time, a full minute went by before she got an answer.

nolaj1994: *ok*

Marnie heaved an enormous sigh of relief, but she knew that feeling would morph into anxiety the moment she saw Nola. When she was in the shower minutes later, she wondered if she had ever before been scared to see Nola.

And then it hit her. Marnie's world wasn't ending at all. It was turning completely upside-down.

Chapter 19

Around 7:30 on Saturday night, Nola sat cross-legged in the backseat of a dark blue Toyota Corolla, fiddling with her shoelaces as if they were strings on her long-lost hoodie. Marnie was all aglow in the front seat, singing along with 96.1 KISS FM and messing up the Spanish parts to a Shakira song, while Mrs. Fitzpatrick kept an eye out for Lizette Levin's house on Morgan Lake.

Nola rolled the window down, and the crisp September air felt soothing as it grazed her forehead and cheeks. The sun had just set over the water so the stars were barely visible, but when she glanced up at the cloudy evening sky, she knew they were still up there.

Mrs. Fitzpatrick pulled into a gravel driveway that led up to a majestic villa with solar panels on the roof and a porch that wrapped around the entire ground floor. Nola tried to focus on those hidden stars instead of her anxiety. Three weeks ago, she could vividly picture what Marnie's birthday party would be like, and it had looked nothing like this — fancy costumes, set inside a home that could be featured on the cover of *Town & Country*, and attended by the coolest Majors in the freshman class.

She also figured she'd be in good spirits after their Friday sleepover, but things still felt weird, especially after their awkward meeting on the school stairs yesterday morning. Marnie had apologized repeatedly for not getting back to her and explained that she forgot to turn her computer off but, for the first time ever, Nola was skeptical of her explanation. Marnie had let her down on more than one occasion over the past few days, and Nola had no idea what to expect from her anymore.

But most of all, Nola had imagined that the excited expression that was on Marnie's face right now would have appeared the moment Nola gave her the handmade bracelet, which was wrapped in elegant purple paper that she bought from Papyrus and tucked in her jeans pocket. However, Nola was waiting for the right moment to give it to her friend, and it just hadn't come upon them yet.

"Can you believe this is happening?" Marnie pulled down the visor and flipped open the tiny makeup mirror so that she could reapply her Hard Candy Lollipop lip gloss. "I'm so glad we decided to have the party here, Nol. It's going to be so much fun!"

Nola gave her a halfhearted smile. She wanted to share in Marnie's enthusiasm — she *really* did — but given everything that had happened up until yesterday, she was terrified of what was on the horizon. Would she feel like an outsider? Would she be able to get past her annoying shyness and act normal for a change? Would her best friend ignore her, like she had been doing a lot lately?

Marnie spun around in her seat and patted Nola on the head affectionately. "Don't worry, okay? You'll be fine."

For a moment, Nola believed her. In fact, there was a fraction of a second where she even saw herself enjoying the murder mystery game and hanging out with the popular kids. But as soon as she spotted Lizette, clad in a glamorous silk pantsuit, and a short forty-something man with tortoiseshell glasses walk out of the house, Nola's skin felt as though it was wrapped in itchy wool. She tried to calm herself by closing her eyes and counting backward from one hundred, but a high-pitched squeal distracted her when she reached eighty-three.

"Happy birthday, chica!" Lizette shrieked as she approached the car with her dad.

Nola swallowed hard as she watched Marnie bounce out of the Toyota joyfully. Marnie and Lizette hugged, then jumped up and down as if they had just scored front-row tickets to *Idols Live* (Marnie had confessed on the way over that both she and Lizette wanted to kiss Ace Young — *blech!*). Nola emerged from the car without much fanfare, and stayed in close proximity to Mrs. Fitzpatrick, where she thought it might be safer.

"It's such a pleasure to meet you," Marnie's mom said, extending her hand gracefully to Mr. Levin. "I've read a few of your books. They were great, especially *Die, Bastard, Die.*"

Mr. Levin shook Mrs. Fitzpatrick's hand but looked down at his shoes. "Oh, well, how nice."

Nola couldn't take her eyes off Lizette, who was staring at her, grimacing. Out of the corner of her eye, Nola saw Marnie mouth the words, "Say something," and that snapped Nola out of her trance. "Hi," she said, her voice weak and wobbly.

Lizette acknowledged Nola with a mere nod. Then she tugged on Marnie's arm and started dragging her toward the house. "Come on, we don't want to keep everyone waiting."

Nola's ears perked up. *Everyone?*

"I'll be writing in my study all night, so no need to worry about the party getting out of hand," Mr. Levin said as he kicked at some gravel with his Brooks Brothers shoes.

Out of hand?

Mrs. Fitzpatrick just smiled. "Of course."

Chills crept up Nola's spine when she saw a patch of fog drift off the lake. Her pulse quickened when she heard an owl hoot and Mr. Levin say something about this house inspiring the disemboweling scene in his most popular novel, *I, Succubus.*

Which couldn't bode well for the evening.

"Nola!" Marnie was on the front porch already, yelling at the top of her lungs. "Hurry up!"

Forget about the forces of evil that were about to descend on Casa Levin. Being the tagalong for the evening was definitely going to be much, much worse.

Mrs. Fitzpatrick got back in her car and drove off while Nola and Mr. Levin strolled toward the house. With each step, Nola noticed that the noise coming from 273 Morgan Lake Road increased a few decibels. What should have sounded like some nice young girls having a murder mystery party actually sounded like P. Diddy and thirty members of his posse having a hot-tub shindig.

Right before they reached the porch, Mr. Levin coughed a bit and said, "Brace yourself."

Oh no, Nola thought as her face flushed red.

But before she could ask what he meant by that, it was obvious. Mr. Levin opened the front door to Par-tay Central. In the huge foyer with a cathedral ceiling were nine girls from PCHS who Nola knew only by face. They were all drinking Diet Cokes and dressed as though they worshipped at the altar of Stella McCartney. When the girls caught sight of Nola, they started whispering and snickering.

This must be some sort of hallucination, she told herself and rubbed her eyes. But when she stopped, the girls were still there. There had to be some mistake. Marnie hadn't said anything about this party being open to the public!

Nola kept her head down and slipped by the foyer girls. She made her way into the rustic, pine-scented living room with hardwood floors, where she was met by an even bigger group of strangers. At least five more girls and ten boys were milling around, chatting with each other and half listening/half dancing to the Raconteurs. She wandered nervously over to a corner and made herself scarce as she tried to scan the crowd for Marnie.

But she didn't have to try for long.

Lizette strolled into the room, a long, sheer pink scarf billowing behind her, with her arm around Marnie. Brynne and Grier — both decked out in their period costumes, which included shimmering sequins and sparkling jewels that might actually be real — followed close behind. Lizette positioned herself and her hangers-on in the center of the room, then got everyone's attention by standing on top of an ottoman and yelling, "Shut your faces, people!"

Once everyone quieted down, Lizette continued.

"Guys, I'd like to welcome you all to Marnie Fitzpatrick's murder mystery birthday party. We're psyched to have you here."

"Of course, we'd be even more psyched if you voted for Marnie for class treasurer in two weeks!" Grier chimed in.

Nola nearly choked on her own tongue. Class treasurer? First of all, Marnie had gotten a C in algebra last year and could barely keep track of her measly allowance. Second of all, she hadn't told Nola anything about being interested in running for a student council position. How could she keep something like that to herself? It was important news, and up until a few days ago, Marnie would have told Nola about it as soon as it happened.

Brynne took her long strand of black pearls and twirled it around in front of her as if it were a propeller and she was about to take off and fly to another level of snottiness. "Grier is going to pass out the game rules and costumes. If anyone has questions, just let Lizette know."

Nola rolled her eyes. She couldn't get over how much everyone worshipped Lizette. *Cult members have more individuality than this,* she thought as Grier milled about and handed out pieces of paper and shopping bags with labels on them.

Before Nola was handed her things, she caught

Marnie's eye. Marnie motioned for Nola to come out from behind the indoor shrubbery, but it was as if her feet were shackled to the radiator. She wasn't able to move even the tiniest muscle. In fact, she wasn't even sure if she was blinking.

Grier pulled the plant leaves to the side and smiled at Nola. "Here ya go," she said, handing her a piece of paper and a Banana Republic bag.

"Thanks," Nola managed to say.

First, she read the instructions of the role-playing game carefully — the last thing she wanted to do was screw up in front of this huge group of people. In fact, screwing up would involve coming out from behind the plant, and that seemed like a stupid thing to do. But as she got through the do's and don'ts, a grin crept over her face. The game actually seemed like fun. Everyone would have a role, and people would be assigned partners so they could look for clues and find the killer. This wasn't so bad.

Then she peered inside the plastic bag and pulled out a dingy gray smock. She reached in farther and out came an apron and a white shower cap-like hat, which had a tag pinned to it. Nola nervously flipped the tag over and read the inscription:

MRS. BILLINGSWORTH, LOYAL SERVANT TO THE TAYLOR FAMILY.

Nola looked up at Marnie again. She was talking with Lizette, holding up a beautiful ink-black fringe-covered flapper dress and giggling. Nola's heart sank when she realized that the person she always thought of as her all-time partner was probably going to pick someone else, someone better, someone who was dressed as a baroness and not as a maid. She'd never felt so overwhelmed as she gazed around the room and saw all the kids that Lizette had brought here, just for Marnie. She stared awestruck at the decorations, the preparations, and the costumes. How could Nola even come close to competing with this?

Lizette clapped her hands together, commanding everyone's attention again. "Okay, now that everyone has read the rules, I'm going to pick a name out of my father's *favorite* top hat — the one he wears to the Metropolitan Opera — and reveal our murder victim."

Nola's breath became short as Brynne handed Lizette the top hat. Some of the boys created a drumroll sound by pounding on the solid oak coffee table in front of the L-shaped tan leather sofa. Lizette dipped into the hat and made some melodramatic faces as other girls cheered her on.

Whatever, Nola thought.

Lizette brought out a folded piece of paper and showed it to Brynne. They broke into a fit of laughter.

Lizette put the paper in her white-beaded purse and snapped it closed. Brynne stood on top of the ottoman and pointed at Nola.

"Mrs. Billingsworth, I regret to inform you that . . . you're *dead!*"

And with that witty and snide remark, the whole room erupted with applause.

Oh please, please-please-please. Nola yanked up her shirt sleeve and saw that bumps were already starting to form on her right forearm. She could feel herself getting queasy and dizzy, too. She was straining to see the person who was coming toward her with a bottle marked with the traces of a Mr. Yuk sticker, as well as the word POISON. At first, she thought it was Lizette coming to finish her off, but then she smelled the scent of Bath & Body Works cucumber melon lotion and knew exactly who it was.

Marnie wedged herself behind the potted plant and stood next to Nola. "Can I talk to you for a sec?"

She nodded her head, hoping this was all a sick, twisted dream and that she'd wake up any minute.

"Are you *hiding* behind this plant?" Marnie asked with concern.

Nola wanted to be brave, but it was no use. She was full-on freaking out. "Yes, I am. How come you didn't tell me all these people were going to be here?"

"I'm just as surprised as you are," Marnie replied. "But isn't it great? Deirdre and Keri-Anne are here! And so are half the kids in our class. It's unbelievable."

The VIP party attendees made no difference to Nola. All she could think about was the satisfied look on Lizette's face when Brynne had announced that Nola was dead — and how Marnie hadn't seemed to notice it at all. "Want to know something else that's unbelievable?" Nola said sharply. "You, running for class treasurer."

Marnie bit her lower lip. "I know. It wasn't something I planned."

Nola scratched at her forearm rapidly. "Well, I just think it's weird that Lizette knew about it and I didn't."

"Are you okay?" Marnie asked while trying to get a closer look at Nola's hives.

But Nola pulled away. This time, she couldn't bring herself to tell Marnie that everything was fine when it wasn't. "No, I'm not okay. I want to go home."

Marnie crossed her arms in front of her chest and sighed heavily. "Why?"

Why? Nola's head spun. Had Marnie just met her? How could she ask, of all things, *why?*

"Um, let's see. Because Lizette just had me whacked!" Nola replied in a loud whisper. "In front of Deirdre and Keri-Anne and everyone else!"

Marnie put her hand over her mouth to stop herself from chuckling. "Nobody *whacked* you, Nola. It was just bad luck."

Nola remembered how Lizette had conveniently put the piece of paper with the victim's name on it in her purse, where no one else could get to it. She shook her head. Why didn't she guess at this setup earlier? "I bet you my name wasn't even *on* that paper. Lizette set me up to be the ugly, stupid corpse maid all along!"

"Get a grip, Nol," Marnie whispered in an annoyed tone. "You're being ridiculous."

Nola put on her maid's hat and tilted it to the side. "Am I? Am I *really*?"

"Yes." Marnie glanced down at her cute black suede pumps and frowned. "And you're ruining my party," she mumbled.

As soon those words hit Nola's ears, she felt her legs turn into instant pudding. Here she was coming up with Lizette–conspiracy theories (which were most likely 100 percent true) instead of making sure Marnie had fun on *her* special day. Even though she was hurting on the inside, she felt that she owed it to her friend to stick around and play dead, because if the situation were reversed, Marnie would do the same thing for Nola . . . right?

"I'm sorry," Nola said, grabbing the poison bottle from Marnie. "Want me to drink this whole thing as punishment?"

Marnie laughed. "It's just a prop."

"Oh, well. Hopefully someone will put me out of my misery," she said, nudging Marnie.

"Think of it this way. Everyone will be so busy looking for the person who killed you that you can spend the rest of the night back here if you want."

Nola started to seriously consider that option, but then Marnie peered out from behind the plant and waved to someone. Nola poked her head out, too, and saw that the someone was Lizette.

Marnie quickly looked back at Nola. "Listen, I know how this whole scene has you bugging out. Would it make you feel better if we met up on the back porch a little bit later and talked for a while?"

Nola breathed a sigh of relief. *There* was the Marnie she knew and loved. "Yes, it would make me feel *a lot* better. Thanks."

Marnie grimaced. "Okay, let's synchronize our watches."

"I'm not wearing a watch," Nola said worriedly.

"It's a figure of speech, Nol. Relax."

"Right. Sorry."

Marnie put her hand on Nola's shoulder. "You and me, on the back porch at eight thirty. Got it?"

"Got it," Nola repeated.

"Great," Marnie said while straightening Nola's hat. "So I'm supposed to tell you to go change into your costume, and then lie down on the floor next to the murder weapon."

Nola gave her a quizzical look. "How long am I supposed to lie there? It could be hours before someone figures out whodunit."

"Well, Lizette's my partner, so I'll ask her." Marnie peeked out from behind the plant again and smiled. "You ready?"

All of a sudden, Nola's mixed feelings of guilt and relief were replaced with the harsh sting of jealousy. She tried to squelch it as best she could, but as Marnie slunk out into the living room and was welcomed into Lizette's circle of friends, the sting felt more like a knife in her back.

Chapter 20

"Get in a little closer!" Grier said cheerily as she aimed her Samsung camera phone at Marnie, Lizette, and Brynne. The girls were striking a group pose and showing off their totally glam ensembles. The rest of the partygoers milled about talking, giggling, dancing, joking, and doing basically everything except hunting down the person who poisoned poor Mrs. Billingsworth.

But Marnie was really the one who was in her own little world. As she stood on Lizette's left side, holding her leg out in front like a Rockette and making a kissy-face, she reveled in the fact that *she* was the guest of honor at this rocking party. Pretty Majors that she'd never even thought of speaking to had come up and wished her a happy birthday or complimented her outfit. Some of the hottest guys in the freshman class had said that they'd vote for her instead of "that Jeremy Atwood creep" because she was "one fresh cheetah" — whatever that meant. It was as if the fancy ball she had wished for when she was five (and obsessed over after seeing the Drew Barrymore movie *Ever After*) had finally come to fruition, and a fairy godmother named Lizette Levin was the one to thank for it all.

"Awwww, this pic is *too cute*," Grier said, smiling.

She skipped over and showed them the JPEG on the screen of her phone.

Lizette wasn't paying much attention, though. She was too busy peering over everyone's heads.

"Oh no, Zee is shoulder-surfing," Brynne said jokingly. "Looking for someone better to talk to?"

"Puh-*lease*," Lizette replied. "I'm just admiring my amazing work."

Marnie smiled. "Everything turned out great, Lizette. I can't thank you enough."

"You're welcome," Lizette said nonchalantly as she turned and gazed out into the crowd again. All of a sudden she lost her composure briefly and squealed, "He showed!"

"Who?" Brynne asked.

"Sawyer Lee," Lizette said, regaining her cool.

Marnie's knees nearly buckled. Sawyer Lee was here? *Her* Sawyer Lee?

Grier clasped her hands together. "How awesome!"

Marnie glanced over at the fireplace and saw Sawyer smiling in her direction. The fake pipe he was holding in his hand made him look so distinguished, even though his blond-tipped spikes were gelled up higher than ever. He'd put on a long tuxedo jacket, but still wore his long baggy jeans and red Vans. Marnie couldn't get over how amazing he looked. But now that Lizette had staked her claim on him, he was totally off-limits, because friendship always came before boys, right?

"Are you going to go over and talk to him?" Brynne asked Lizette.

"Don't be such a dope, Brynne. He's supposed to come to *me*. And he will, eventually," Lizette replied confidently.

Marnie didn't have a doubt in her mind that that would happen. Lizette was the epitome of fabulosity. There was no way Sawyer would be able to resist her. In fact, he was already winking at Lizette and waving her over. How unfair was that?

But as soon as Marnie began contemplating the possible coupling of Lizette and Sawyer, she heard a loud squirting sound that startled everyone in the room. She turned in the direction of the refreshments table and saw Nola covered in A&W root beer. Apparently, the two-liter bottle had burst like a geyser when Nola had tried to open it.

Everyone laughed while Nola slipped away into the kitchen, soaked with soda. Marnie just bowed her head in shame.

"That girl is *such* a dweeb," Brynne sneered.

Lizette neither agreed nor disagreed with Brynne. She just crossed her arms over her chest and rolled her eyes.

Marnie felt her hands go numb. How could Nola keep

embarrassing herself like this, and by proxy, embarrassing Marnie? If Nola weren't so anxious all the time, maybe she wouldn't be such a klutz. However Marnie tried to rationalize it, though, certain things were becoming all too clear. No matter how much Marnie took care of and encouraged her, Nola was never going to change.

"Well, since she's the maid, I suppose she'll clean up the floor," Brynne added snarkily.

But that didn't mean Marnie still wouldn't throw down for her.

Oh, I'm going to teach this girl a lesson she'll never forget. Marnie was about to lunge at Brynne when Lizette grabbed her arm.

"Hey, someone's here to see you," she said, gesturing to the living room entrance.

Marnie gasped. There stood Dane Harris, decked out in a jacket and tie, hands in his pockets, hair absolutely perfect, smile positively stunning, staring straight at her. The sight of him temporarily wiped Sawyer Lee from her memory bank.

Lizette leaned over and whispered in her ear, "I hear he really likes you."

"He does?" Marnie asked breathlessly.

She checked out her reflection in the nearest bay window. Her heart skipped when she noticed Dane was lurking behind her. She spun around to greet him and all of her friends scattered, so it was just the two of them.

"Hey there. Sorry I'm late," Dane said, adjusting his tie so that it hung lower around his neck.

"What took you so long?" she asked with a flip of her hair and a knowing smile.

"I'll tell you, but only if we get out of here," he replied with an equally sly grin.

Without hesitation, Marnie took his hand and led him to the door.

Five minutes later, Marnie and Dane were walking around the lake, side-by-side and close enough that she could feel the sleeve of his tweed jacket rub against her bare arm. They'd only been in each other's company for a few minutes, but it was the longest stretch of time Marnie had spent with him yet, and she wasn't about to waste this opportunity to do anything other than flirt.

Right now, Dane was talking about how Mr. Levin's lake house stacked up to his mother's vacation spot near the Chesapeake Bay. But Marnie's mind was occupied with other things, like the way Dane's burgundy tie made him look as if he'd just come from TA-ing a class at Marist College. Even though they were strolling along in the moonlight, she noticed that he'd parted his hair differently and that there was a tiny scar under his left earlobe. She counted in her head each time Dane gently moved her to the side when a car came down the dark, winding road, or when he smiled at her, then quickly looked away. Marnie didn't understand how Lizette could call him dull or how anyone could think he was some party-obsessed player. He was the perfect blend of hotness, sweetness, flirtiness, and flawlessness.

As they came to a small pier that reached out into the tepid, still water, Marnie felt her breath catch in her throat. Her self-confidence melted into nervousness, and not just because she might be minutes away from kissing Dane Harris. It was also because it had been a while since she had kissed anyone. What if she wasn't good at it anymore? She tried to clear her head by pulling her shoulders back and concentrating on creating a straight line with her spine.

Dane sat on the edge of the dock and let his legs dangle. He turned around when he noticed that Marnie was about ten paces behind him. "I won't let you fall in," he said, his eyes twinkling.

"I'm not worried about that," Marnie said, smiling.

"Then why are you all the way over there?" he asked.

Marnie could feel the hairs on her arms stand up. She slowly approached Dane, listening as each one of her footsteps disturbed the peaceful silence. She sat down next to him, but not too close. She wanted to be able to look over and take him all in.

Dane's cheeks were pink from the cold and when he exhaled, Marnie could see the thin outline of his breath. "You must be freezing," he said, gesturing toward Marnie's itsy-bitsy dress.

Strangely enough, she hadn't experienced the slightest chill. "I'm fine."

His eyebrows arched. "Really?"

"Yeah, in fact, this is perfect weather for running," Marnie said, swinging her legs back and forth like a little girl.

"Well, since we're just sitting, I'm going to give you my coat." Dane peeled it off, leaned over, and draped it around Marnie's shoulders. He ran his right hand from the nape of her neck down to her lower back and left it lingering there.

Marnie sat on her hands so that Dane wouldn't see them shaking. She glanced up to the sky and tried to stargaze, hoping that he would make a move when she wasn't paying attention. But there were too many thick clouds covering the constellations, and Dane's hand remained on the small of her back.

"This is going to sound lame, but I don't care. Are you wishing upon a star?"

She turned her head and stared into his shining green eyes. "Well, I *am* the birthday girl."

Dane shifted a little closer to Marnie and his hand moved to her waist, which literally made her toes curl. "That's right. So what are you wishing for?"

Marnie leaned in so that she could whisper in his ear, her lips lightly sweeping over his neck. "It's a secret."

Dane started laughing, his forehead briefly leaning against Marnie's. "Where have I heard that before?"

She saw the way the corners of his lips turned up when he laughed and had to do everything in her power not to leap on him right then and there. "I can't believe you want me to tell you my birthday wish. If I did that, it wouldn't come true!"

"Silly me." Dane tucked a stray lock of blonde hair behind Marnie's ear and then turned his gaze to the lake. "It's really pretty out here, isn't it?"

"It kind of reminds me of —" Marnie stopped mid-sentence. When she realized where this chain of thoughts would lead her, she wanted to take them back.

"Reminds you of what?" Dane was looking at her again. This was going to make it even harder.

Before she could get ahold of herself, Marnie was choking back tears. "It just reminds me of these camping trips my family used to take. You know, when I was

little and before my parents were divorced and everything."

You are such a blubbering idiot! she thought. *You're going
to ruin your mascara and look like a huge dork! Talk about
something else!* Anything *else!*

Dane didn't seem to be concerned about her makeup,
though. Instead of backing away, he put his arm around
her and gave her a light squeeze. "Good times, huh?"

Marnie closed her eyes and thought for a second
about where her dad might be tonight. But luckily
she managed to avoid emotional overload and replied,
"The best."

"Well, here's an idea. How about I give you one
more thing to put in the Best Times column?" Dane
asked as his hands cupped her face and his soft reddish
lips grazed the tip of her nose.

She knew that if she moved one more millimeter,
they'd be kissing. But thankfully she didn't have to
move. It was as if Dane knew what her birthday wish
had been before she'd even made it.

When Marnie closed her eyes this time, Dane's
mouth was pressed against hers. It didn't occur to her
that she barely knew him, or that a breeze had picked
up, scattering newly fallen leaves around the edge of the
lake. The only thing she could think about was how
amazing this felt — her arms resting on his shoulders,

his hands on her face, her pulse racing racing racing. It couldn't get any better than this.

Dane came up for air briefly and gave her a smile that made her giddy. "Hope it came true, Marnie."

Her heart took off like a hot air balloon, and before she could really absorb what was happening between them, he was kissing her again until she couldn't think about anything else, not even the friend she was very, very late to meet.

Chapter 21

Nola didn't have to look at a clock to know that Marnie had blown her off. She'd been sitting at the picnic table on Lizette's deck for a long, long time, anxiously waiting as people from the party came out to get a better view of the lake. Nola swallowed each time the sliding door opened and someone else invaded her territory. But everyone acted as though Nola was invisible, much to her relief.

A light mist of rain began to drizzle — the kind of rain that doesn't really require an umbrella, but is wet nonetheless. Everyone on the deck had wandered back into the house, except for Nola. She stayed perched on the edge of the picnic table, with her feet on the bench in front of her, gazing at the water. Her thoughts were tumbling. How could Marnie blatantly burn her like this? What on earth was happening to them?

Nola fished out her cell phone from her pocket and stared at it. She wished she could call Matt and ask him to ride over on his bike and pick her up. She scrolled through her list of contacts and landed on MATT H.

She was about to hit the DIAL button when the sliding door flew open again. Nola put her phone away and turned her head to see who was joining her. She wanted nothing more than to scale the drainpipe when she witnessed Lizette and Sawyer Lee stepping out onto the deck.

What is going on here? Nola thought.

Sawyer walked to the edge of the deck and dug around in the pocket of his jeans without noticing Nola's presence. But her hopes of getting away undetected were dashed when Lizette locked the door from the outside and made a beeline for Sawyer. A few seconds later, Nola saw him pull Lizette close to him, lean in, and kiss her.

Nola wanted to turn her head and stare at something else, like the half moon that was dangling in the sky above, but she couldn't seem to turn away from the smooch-fest happening before her.

For the next few seconds, Nola wondered whether or not she should tell Marnie about what she'd seen. Sure, Marnie seemed really into Dane these days, but she'd been obsessed with her number one crush since the dawn of grammar school. And now he was swapping spit with the Almighty Lizette! Nola was almost sure that Marnie would go berserk if she knew — Nola had once mentioned that she liked the shorts Sawyer was wearing, and Marnie's skin had turned a shade of bright red that Nola thought only she herself could achieve.

She was so wrapped up in her thoughts that she almost didn't notice the pinching sensation on her ankle. But then there were two more so she couldn't ignore it. *Definitely mosquitoes.* Slapping her leg as hard as she could was a reflex, but it got the attention of a certain someone whose face was glued to a guy who lived in ankle biters.

Nola sat motionless as she watched Lizette glare at her.

"Be right back," Lizette said to Sawyer before stepping away and turning toward Nola.

As Lizette moved in quickly, all Nola could do was prepare for the beat-down that the hostess with the mostest was about to give her.

"What are you doing out here? Spying?" Lizette snapped and put her hands on her hips.

Nola was at a loss. She couldn't say "waiting for Marnie" because that would sound pathetic. She searched her brain for some excuse that would make sense, but all she could come up with was, "Um, I don't know."

Thankfully, a loud series of knocks came to the rescue. Lizette and Nola flinched in unison. Sawyer tried to act casual.

"What if it's my dad?" Lizette murmured. She ran to the door as if someone had set her hair on fire, but breathed a sigh of relief when she saw who was standing on the other side. "It's just Dane and Marnie," she said while unlocking the door.

Dane strode in with this wide mischievous grin on his face, and even though Marnie was wearing his jacket, she looked a little disheveled. Now Nola knew why Marnie hadn't shown up as she'd promised. She and Dane had been kissing, too! Nola couldn't believe it. First, she had to witness Lizette and Sawyer, and now she was being ditched for Dane!

"You dudes are such losers," Sawyer said, relaxing his shoulders. "We thought you were Zee's father."

As for Marnie, she hadn't even acknowledged Nola's existence yet.

"So did you show Marnie *around*?" Lizette teased.

Dane raised his eyebrows and glanced at Marnie, who giggled as if she were a preschooler. "Maybe."

"Let's go back in, it's getting cold out here," Lizette said, rubbing her arms.

"I'm not cold at all," Marnie said slyly.

Nola rolled her eyes.

"Come on, Marnie. I want to show you these *sick* motorcycle boots in my room," Lizette said, nodding toward the sliding-glass door.

They started to walk away, so Nola tried clearing

her throat loudly to get Marnie's attention. It worked. Marnie turned around somewhat and waved excitedly to Nola. Then she mouthed the words, "Be right back."

Nola's face fell as Marnie went into the house. How could she be this cruel?

Sawyer headed toward the door, but Dane didn't budge from his spot against the railing.

Nola realized that she had to go inside, too, or risk being trapped out there with the vice president. She tried not to appear freaked out, but she leaped up from the picnic table so fast, it seemed as though she'd been launched into the air by a catapult.

But then Dane cut her off at the pass. He locked the door and blocked it so that she couldn't get around him. "Where are you going?"

Nola gulped. "Uh . . . to the bathroom?"

He grabbed an empty Coke can off the deck railing. "If you're the maid, aren't you supposed to be at my beck and call?" He held out the can and shook it as if she was supposed to throw it out for him.

This was the last straw. Nola was sick of being such a spineless wimp. If she didn't say or do something now, she just wouldn't be able to respect herself.

"Well, I'm on a break, *jerk!*" Nola blurted and then

shoved him aside. She tried to unlock the door but she was so agitated that her hands were fumbling with the handle.

Then Dane came up from behind, putting both arms around her so that his hands were on top of her hands. "You have to push in this button and pull up on the handle at the same time," he said. Once the door opened, he backed away.

Nola didn't even bother to say thanks. She just bolted into the house. She wanted to tell Marnie about Lizette and Sawyer right away, before she lost her nerve. If only she could get to talk to her privately.

But that wasn't going to be easy. Instead of going up to Lizette's room to ogle her "sick motorcycle boots," Marnie was in a big circle of people, including Brynne, Grier, and a few other Majors. Nola was not an expert at social graces and she had no idea how to steal Marnie away without seeming totally clingy. However, she took a deep breath, wiggled her way through the crowd, and broke through the circle so that she was standing next to Marnie.

Nola tapped her on the shoulder and smirked. "So did you have a good time tonight?" She knew her voice was loaded with sarcasm, but she felt entitled to be upset.

"Kind of," Marnie replied, keeping her attention on what everyone else around her was saying.

Nola's blood boiled. She couldn't even get two seconds of Marnie's time anymore? "I think I remember you promising that you'd meet me on the back deck at eight thirty."

Marnie spun around so she was fully facing Nola. "I know. I feel so bad. It's just that —"

"Dane Harris asked to 'show you around'?" Nola interjected.

"Yeah," Marnie said, her mouth suddenly turning into a big smile. She leaned in and whispered, "And guess what? He kissed me. Can you believe it? I kissed Dane Harris!"

Nola knew that she was supposed to muster up some excitement here, but after her weird encounter with Dane a few seconds ago, she just couldn't. "That's great," she said flatly.

Marnie was no longer smiling anymore. In fact, she appeared irritated and ready to stomp off in a huff. "I *said* I was sorry about before."

Nola slouched forward and sighed. She didn't want to hear any more of Marnie's apologies. She just wanted things to go back to the way they were. "Marn, I need to talk to you about something important."

"What is it?"

Nola looked around to make sure no one was listening. "Not here. Can we go back outside?"

"Nola, Lizette's about to bring the cake out. Can't it wait?" Marnie bit her lip.

"Actually, it can't," Nola said urgently. She spoke softly into Marnie's ear. "It's about Lizette."

"What? I can't hear you over the music."

Nola sighed. She cleared her throat and spoke up. "It's about Lizette. And Sawyer Lee. They were —"

Without warning, Lizette appeared right next to Nola. "Doing what?" Lizette asked.

Marnie's eyes grew wide with fear. Nola was used to her best friend bailing her out during moments like this, but Marnie just stood there, frozen.

Nola swallowed hard. She had to do some back-pedaling — real fast. "Yeah, um, I was just going to say I saw you both on the deck earlier. That's it. Pretty boring story, actually."

"Uh-huh." Lizette didn't seem convinced in the least.

Nola could tell that Marnie was really embarrassed because she kept her eyes lowered and was fidgeting with some of the fringe on her dress. It was as though she'd evicted Marnie from the House of Cool and shipped her off to the Island of Dorks.

"I'm going to get my dad so we can serve the cake," Lizette said with ice in her voice. Then she turned around and walked briskly toward the kitchen.

Marnie grabbed Nola's arm hard and yanked her over to an unoccupied corner of the living room. "What's gotten into you?" she demanded.

"I'm sorry." Nola was so upset she was trembling. "It's just that I saw them kissing outside."

"So?"

So? That's all Marnie had to say? Nola was caught off guard. She was expecting a huge, angry reaction. "Well, um, I thought you'd want to know about it, you know, because Sawyer is —"

"I couldn't care less, Nol," Marnie interrupted. "I wish you'd kept your mouth shut. I feel like such a loser."

"I didn't mean to —"

"You never mean to." Marnie seemed truly exasperated. "Lizette is my friend and she can kiss whoever she wants. Okay?"

Nola was stunned when she heard Marnie call Lizette her friend. When Lizette brought out the cake and hugged Marnie after she blew out the candles, Nola went from stunned to shocked. She couldn't watch their chumminess anymore, which is why she called Mrs. Fitzpatrick and told her she needed a ride home.

Twenty minutes later, Marnie's mom pulled up in front of 13618 Willow Bend. Nola stared at the front porch of

her house. She had always thought that it looked gran-
diose and palace-like, but now that she'd seen Lizette's
tricked-out lake house, her home seemed tiny and plain
in comparison.

"I'm sorry you're not feeling well, Nola," Mrs.
Fitzpatrick said, patting her leg. "I thought you'd be
sleeping over with Marnie."

Nola undid her seat belt and gathered her things off
the passenger-side floor. "I'll be okay. I probably ate
some bad Cheez-Its, that's all."

"Well, I hope that you had fun up until then." When
Mrs. Fitzpatrick smiled, Nola noticed for the first time
how much Marnie and her mom looked alike. Same
nose. Same eyes. Same chin. Marnie always wanted to
look like Erin, but now Nola couldn't see why. Marnie's
mom was so pretty.

"Could you do me a favor, Mrs. Fitzpatrick?" Nola
asked while reaching into her pocket.

"Sure, hon."

She took out the delicately wrapped box and put it
in Mrs. Fitzpatrick's hand. "I didn't have the chance to
give Marnie her present."

"Oh, how sweet," she said. "I'll make sure that she
gets it."

"Thanks." Nola opened the car door and got out.
"Good night."

She watched Mrs. Fitzpatrick drive down the street and around the corner. She sat down on the porch steps and watched the midnight wind bend tree branches until she got sleepy. Then she went inside to dream of happy birthdays gone by.

Chapter 22

Early on Sunday afternoon, Marnie threw open the screen door to her house and skipped into the living room without so much as a "hey, how are ya?" to her mom, who was busy in the kitchen, tossing pieces of fruit and ice into a blender. Lizette and her dad had just dropped Marnie off and she wanted to hop on the computer to write about her fabulous lake house/murder mystery/ sleepover birthday party in her journal before she forgot any of the details. She threw her overnight bag on the floor and took off her favorite vintage jean jacket, then plopped down on the desk chair.

"Sweetheart, do you want a smoothie?" her mom called out.

Marnie typed in her password to unlock the folder she kept her journal in and began a new file — MY 14TH B-DAY. "No thanks, I had brunch at Lizette's."

"Wow, sounds fancy," her mom shouted over the loud puree cycle.

She started her new entry with a top ten list of high-lights from yesterday.

1) Kissing Dane! (unbelievable kisser, like way better than stupid Weston)

2) Walking into the lake house and seeing all the cool people Lizette invited to celebrate with me! (It was so surreal, like one of those dreams where you're flying and feeling amazing. I still can't believe it actually happened, but it did!)

3) Kissing Dane! (This is worth two of the top spots. That's how great it was.)

4) When Keri-Anne was asked who the prettiest girl in the room was during our late night Truth or Dare session, she said, "Duh, Marnie, of course." (Even though she was tight with Erin, I had no idea Keri-Anne even knew my name, let alone thought I was pretty!)

In the middle of writing her list, Marnie heard the *ping* noise that indicated that she had a new e-mail. She saved her document, reduced the window, and opened up her mailbox. She grinned when she saw that it was a Hallmark e-card from her father. She clicked on the link and watched as Hoops and Yoyo sang "Happy Birthday," laughing as they belted it completely out of tune. Then the message came on the screen:

Dear Marnie-bird,
Hope you had a great time at your lake house party,
my little girl! Sorry this is getting to you late—I've
been so busy apartment hunting. Anyway, enjoy
the iTunes gift certificate and the rest of your 14th
year. See you soon!

I love you,
Dad

Marnie read the message at least five times before her
mom came up alongside her and held out a small box
wrapped in gorgeous purple paper and a gold ribbon.

"It's from Nola. She said she didn't have the chance
to give it to you," her mom said quickly, then ran back
to the kitchen for more smoothie-making.

Oh no, I'm going to lose it, Marnie thought. If her dad's
e-mail didn't bring her to tears, a gift from Nola would
certainly send her over the edge, especially after what
had happened between them last night.

Still, as she undid the gold ribbon, she remembered
how hell-bent Nola had been on having a horrible time.
She'd spent the evening *hiding* instead of getting to know
people and being herself. And then she got caught talking about Lizette behind her back. That was absolutely
mortifying! Thankfully, Lizette didn't mention it all night,
although Marnie wasn't surprised — Lizette was pretty

unflappable. Still, Nola had made herself look really bad, and Marnie was harboring anger over it even now.

Marnie shook her head and tried to get rid of her negative thoughts. Nola had been nice enough to give this package to her mom, even though she'd left the party upset. That had to mean something, right? Maybe there wasn't too much harm done.

Marnie gently peeled back the paper and lifted the lid of a yellow cardboard box. She had to catch her breath when she saw a gorgeous handmade bracelet nestled on top of a small square of cotton. She picked it up and felt the blue, purple, and magenta beads with her fingers. It was the most incredible piece Nola had ever made, and she'd given it to her. *To her.*

Then she noticed there was a tiny envelope attached to the cotton. She put the bracelet on her left wrist and tore the envelope open. Marnie felt tears come to her eyes as she read Nola's note, which was written in messy calligraphy (she had been practicing all summer long and apparently still couldn't get it quite right).

For Marnie, my kindred spirit.
I'd be lost without our friendship.

LYLAS,
N

Marnie was so overwhelmed with conflicting emotions that she shut down her PC, grabbed all her things, and bounded up the stairs to her room, taking the steps two at a time.

She immediately flopped down on her bed and reached for her iPod shuffle. She put in her earbuds and tried to clear her head by listening to music, but she couldn't stop thinking about Nola's note.

I'd be lost without our friendship. Marnie knew she should have been honored or touched to read those words, but instead she was kind of . . . angry. How could Nola give her such a guilt trip on her birthday? Didn't she realize how bad that would make Marnie feel? Marnie had to ask herself why this sweet sentiment was making her feel so awful.

She hated coming to the same realization over and over again. Marnie was growing out of their friendship, and knowing that Nola would be lost without it made her ache with remorse.

There was a knock at the door. Marnie took out her earbuds and said, "Come in."

She was expecting her mom, which was why she gasped when Lizette Levin walked in, wearing a cut-up black T-shirt, an orange terry-cloth mini, and Burberry rain boots. Marnie hadn't had a chance to hide all the embarrassing things in her room, like her stuffed animal collection, or put any of her dirty clothes in her hamper. She glanced around and saw a bunch of other flaws that might catch Lizette's eye — the hand-me-down furniture, the outlet store curtains, the Martha Stewart bedding sold exclusively at Kmart. Marnie had seen firsthand how Lizette lived, and it was nothing like this.

"You left this on the back seat," Lizette said, holding up her pink Razr phone. "And since I gave Dane your number, I doubt you want to miss any calls."

This news made Marnie forget she lived on earth, let alone in the middle-class section of Poughkeepsie. She jumped up and threw her arms around Lizette. "You rock!"

"Whatever, the guy practically got down on his knees and begged me for it," Lizette said, hugging her back. "What did you do to him anyway?"

Marnie flopped back down on her bed, trying not to think about the paint that was peeling on her walls. "Are you staying for a while?"

Lizette walked over to Marnie's mirror, where pictures of Marnie and Nola were tucked in the edge of the frame. She began inspecting them one by one. "Yeah, my dad drove me here and dropped me off. So I have plenty of time to hear all the details."

She laughed. "There's not much to tell."

"That's a pity," Lizette said as she pulled out one photo and examined it closely. "I was hoping to hear that he was a good kisser."

Marnie raised her eyebrow. "I thought you said he was dull."

Lizette spun around so fast her ponytail almost whipped her in the face. "I changed my mind."

"Well, he's an *amazing* kisser, actually." Marnie fell back on her bed and stretched her arms over her forehead. "I mean, everything was perfect."

"You're lucky." Lizette put the picture back and then sat on the edge of Marnie's bed. "Good kissers are so rare."

"I know!" It was so refreshing to talk with Lizette about boys and kissing. Nola didn't have much experience and therefore never had much interest in talking about the fun specifics and mechanics of it all.

"So I have something to tell you," Lizette said mysteriously.

Marnie was intrigued. "What?"

"I kissed Sawyer Lee last night."

It was strange — Marnie already knew this, but somehow when the words came out of Lizette's mouth, she actually winced. But Marnie knew better than to let on that something was wrong. "That's awesome."

Lizette grinned knowingly. "Nola told you, didn't she?"

There was no use in pretending. "Yeah, she did. Sorry."

"Well, why was she so eager to tell you in the first place?" Lizette asked curiously. "Do you like him or something?"

Marnie knew that this was dodgy territory. If she told Lizette that Sawyer was number two (for the time being) on her Crush List, it might really upset her. Sure, Marnie would rather Lizette didn't like Sawyer, but did it even matter? She had Dane, and Dane was unmatchable.

"No way," Marnie said, giving Lizette a playful shove. "Nola's just . . . you know."

"Really weird?" Lizette answered.

Marnie was only able to shrug.

Suddenly Lizette's eyes widened and her mouth went agape. "Hold on — that bracelet is *so fierce!*"

Marnie looked down at her left hand and smiled. "Isn't it great?"

"It's hot, *really* hot," Lizette said, peeling it off Marnie's wrist and putting it on her own. "Did you get this on Prince Street? I see this stuff in Manhattan all the time, but nothing as sweet as this."

Marnie swallowed hard. If she said that Nola made it, Lizette would probably make a face and take it off as if it were a smelly diaper. She had come this far with Lizette, why risk messing it up? However, she couldn't come out and lie about the bracelet's origin either, so she just nodded her head.

"Wow, I love it." Lizette got up and admired herself in Marnie's mirror, posing with her hands on her hips.

"It looks fab on you," Marnie said. It clashed with everything on Lizette, but it was still true.

"Would you mind if I borrowed it?"

Marnie flinched as soon as she realized what she'd been asked. If she said no, Lizette might think she was some sort of possessive, selfish jerk who didn't trust her. After all Lizette had done for Marnie last night, how could there be any answer other than yes? On the other hand, this bracelet was a special gift from Nola, a gift that was supposed to symbolize the friendship Nola would be lost without.

Argh.

Lizette wandered back over to the bed. "I promise to be supercareful with it."

Marnie searched Lizette's face for any hint of insincerity, but there was none. "Okay."

"Thanks, Marn," Lizette said, delighted. "Hey, want to walk to Bartlett Park and watch some hot guys play touch football?"

Marnie's Razr phone buzzed and she flipped it open

to check out a new text message from an unfamiliar number.

R U COMING 2 THE PARK? —D

Marnie looked up at Lizette, who was now wearing a devious smile in addition to Nola's bracelet. Was there anything this girl couldn't do?

"What are we waiting for?" Marnie asked. "Let's go."

Chapter 23

"Hey, you found me!"

Matt was tending to his bike on the lawn of his modest Cape Cod–style house on Ridge Road when Nola arrived with her heavy book bag in tow. He was wearing a pair of beat-up stonewashed jeans with a hole in the right knee and a navy-blue shirt covered in grease stains. The sun was summer-strong this afternoon, causing beads of sweat to form on his forehead and dampen some strands of his hair. Nola was so enchanted by the sight of him she was barely able to squeak out a hello.

"Did you beam yourself over or something? I didn't see your parents' car drive up," Matt said as he finished oiling the chain on his bike and wiped his hands on his knees.

Nola blushed. She had told her mom that she was going to study at Marnie's, but had taken the bus here instead. The last thing she needed was her mom getting all up in her business, especially after the weekend she'd had. "Oh, my mom is at work, so I just used mass transit," she explained.

"That must have taken you forever," he said. "You're

probably thirsty. Come on, let me get you an ice-cold orange soda."

Nola took a deep breath and followed Matt inside. They walked through a long, dimly lit hallway to the kitchen, which was bright and airy, yet quite small. He opened the fridge, grabbed two cans of Sunkist, and tossed one at her. Lucky for Nola, she lived with two projectile-throwing-obsessed brothers, so she caught it with just one hand.

"Nice reflexes," Matt said.

"Thanks." She opened the can and some of the fizz overflowed the top, so she had to slurp it up before any dripped on the floor or on her favorite pair of tan flare-leg jeans.

Matt took a few gulps and made a theatrical *"ahhh"* sound. "So, do you want the grand tour?"

Nola tugged on the hem of her white cotton crewneck nervously. "Will your parents mind us poking around the house?"

"Well, my dad's recording on the Lower East Side and I have no idea when he'll be back, so it's fine." Matt went to the kitchen sink and scrubbed his hands furiously.

"Recording?"

"Yeah, he's a session musician. Today he's laying down some mandolin tracks on this bluegrass album," he explained while drying off his hands on a towel. "But who knows how long it's going to take. He keeps weird hours."

Nola's stomach suddenly got queasy. It seemed that there was no adult supervision in *any* part of this house. And Matt was walking toward her with an odd look on his face, like he could read her mind and see how anxious she was — as well as excited.

He was standing no more than a few inches in front of her when he said, "Sorry I didn't give you one of these when you came in, but I was dirty." Then he wrapped her in the warmest, tightest hug ever. Nola closed her eyes and inhaled — instead of Axe body spray, he now smelled of Coppertone sunblock, antibacterial soap, and Florida oranges.

Mmmmm, delicious.

He pulled away and smiled. "Okay, now on with the tour."

By now, Nola couldn't care less about seeing the rest of Matt's house. All she wanted to do was fly with him to some remote island in the Pacific. But the best thing was that she didn't have to be in a special place in order to have a good time with Matt. And best of all, he was making her forget all about Marnie's awful birthday party, and the fact that Marnie hadn't called to say thank you for her present.

Over the next few minutes, Matt showed Nola the hot spots of the Heatherly household by pointing out certain items that had sentimental value. There was the living room sofa in which Matt had torn a gigantic hole while wrestling with his cat, Bouncer; the third spindle on the stairs railing Matt accidentally knocked out with a baseball bat; the SpongeBob SquarePants shower curtain Matt had bought with his paper route money; and of course, the famous Ziggy Stardust poster that hung on his wall.

Nola sat down on Matt's bed and looked around in awe. There were amps and bass guitars everywhere. CDs were strewn about the floor. "Wow, you are such a . . . boy," she blurted out.

"Yeah, well, that's how my dad raised me," Matt said, chuckling.

There was something about the way he said, "how my *dad* raised me" — that got Nola thinking. She replayed the tour of the house in her mind and realized there wasn't anything feminine about it. No pastels, no lace fabrics, no scented candles, no knick-knacks, and no picture of family and friends, with the exception of a snapshot in Matt's room. It appeared to be of a pretty middle-aged woman, but Nola could barely see the photo because it was tucked behind a stack of music magazines. Other than that, there was nothing to indicate that Matt's mom lived here, or ever had.

"Don't get too comfy. There's one more thing I want to show you." Matt took Nola by the hands and pulled her off his bed, then led her down the upstairs hallway until they were standing underneath a square door on the ceiling with a rope tied to it. He grabbed hold of the rope and yanked hard. Attached to the other side of the door was a ladder, which Matt extended fully so it reached the ground. "After you," he said.

Nola eyed him suspiciously. "Why don't you go first?"

"Because the safety latch on this ladder is kind of shoddy and —"

"Say no more," she said, quickly climbing up the ladder as if it were about to snap. When she got to the top, she had to crouch down because the ceiling was sort of low. But as she glanced around, she knew that this space was a window into Matt's heart.

He came up behind her and put his arm around her shoulder. "Pretty rad, huh?"

The attic was actually a small recording studio, complete with audio equipment, enough instruments to start a twelve-piece band, and soundproof insulation.

Nola walked over to the drum set, hunching forward

a little so she didn't hit her head on one of the beams. She tapped her fingers on one of the cymbals and listened to the crisp sound it made.

"My dad and I had all this stuff in the basement, but then we had some flooding problems, so we had to move everything up here." Matt wove through the gear and sat down on the stool behind the drum set. He picked up the sticks and started banging a rhythm out that got Nola tapping her Skechers on the floor.

"So can you play all these instruments?" she asked.

"Yep, my dad taught me mostly," Matt shouted over the loud beat, then he stopped cold. "Wanna try?"

Nola shook her head. "No thanks."

"You can't get to the honey without smokin' the hive."

"What?"

Matt patted his lap. "Just have a seat, and I'll show you how it's done."

She glanced down at Matt's legs. There was no way she could get that close to him and not melt into a pile of girl-mush. So she wandered over to the wind section and started looking at a saxophone. But then she imagined Matt's mouth touching the reed, and her eyes began to burn. She put her hands over her face and tried to compose herself.

"Hey, Nola, come over here and try this."

"Oh no, not the cowbell," she said, laughing.

"The cowbell is where it's at, baby!" Matt hit it a few times and made a few obnoxious '80s hair-metal faces. Nola started to laugh so he kept going. "Oh yeah! Bring it on home!"

Soon she was laughing so hard she thought she might choke. She dashed over to Matt, snatched the cowbell and the drum stick, and held them behind her back.

"The cowbell was meant to be mistreated!" Matt shouted with a fake Southern accent. "Make it hurt so good!"

"You want it? You got it!" Without thinking very much about how she looked, or anything else, Nola gave into Matt's urging and started hitting the cowbell, swinging her hips in time with the clanking. Matt kept cheering her on, saying, "Go, baby, go!" until she was dancing around, striking it like a maniac. Matt applauded when she tripped over a wire on the floor and fell down, which ended her live show. Needless to say, by then she was curled up in a fetal position, dying of laughter.

Matt was standing over her, looking down with approval. "Were you this much fun at Marnie's party?"

Nola glanced away and tried to catch her breath. "No, I wasn't." She thought for a minute about confiding in Matt about what had happened. He seemed so nice and levelheaded. Maybe he'd be able to provide some nugget of wisdom that would put everything into perspective and make all her worries disappear. There were a lot of things she wanted to learn about him, too, like if he had really gotten suspended from Arlington, and what had happened to his mother. She wanted to know it all.

He extended a hand. Nola reached out with hers and before he could help her up, she pulled him down on the floor with her. They both broke into a fit of laughter that had them rolling around, clutching their sides, and gasping for air.

"Wow," Matt said, still chuckling hard. "You've got to teach that move to my girlfriend."

A sudden stabbing pain spread throughout Nola's body.

What did he just say?

"Riley's always putting up with my BS," Matt continued. "She needs a line of defense."

Nola's head was now feeling like a bubble that was about to burst. How could Matt have a *girlfriend*? He'd never mentioned this Riley before!

"Does she go to Central?" Nola asked, her voice wavering.

"Nah, we met on her MySpace blog, Riley Finnegan's Wake. She's really into music, like me. In fact, she made the video I showed you." He got off the floor and stretched his arms above his head. "Anyway, Rye lives in Jersey, so now we're doing the long-distance thing."

Riley Finnegan . . . RF . . . RF Forever, Nola thought. *I'm gonna be sick.*

"Um, are you okay?" Matt asked, looking curious.

"Why?"

"You're still lying on the ground."

Nola knew that she wasn't okay at all. She needed to get out of here and fast. "Actually, I'm feeling a little . . . crampy."

My life is over.

"Oh. Well, do you want to crash in my room for a bit?"

Matt was being way too sweet, so naturally, Nola felt even worse. She staggered to her feet. "No, I think I'm just going to head home."

"You sure? It's a long ride back," he said.

She swallowed hard. "I'll be fine."

But Matt was right. The ride home was long. Long enough for Nola to call Marnie three times and leave messages that included, "It's me. Please call me back, this is urgent"; "Me again. I need to talk to you, Marn. It's really important"; and "Where are you? Why aren't you answering me?" But all the messages were met with silence.

An hour later, Nola got off at the bus stop three blocks from her house. As she dragged her feet along the sidewalk, she kept thinking of how she'd been warned about Matt and that she probably should have listened and stayed clear of him. But then again, he hadn't done anything except be nice to her. She had so many confusing feelings juggling around in her mind, and there was only one person who could really help her make sense of it all.

But that person was nowhere to be found.

Suddenly Nola's phone vibrated in her bag. She dug through it and picked up her cell. She had a text message from Marnie.

OUT W/ DH & LL! TTYL. PROMISE.

It was then that Nola's blood practically froze. Not only had she been ditched yet again, but she no longer believed that Marnie would keep any of her promises. When Nola entered her house, she angrily switched off her phone and vowed to give Marnie Fitzpatrick the coldest shoulder of her life.

However, Nola might have decided otherwise had she not missed the following message:

BTW, TX 4 THE BRACELET! SO PRETTY! U R THE BESTEST! LYLAS! XOXO

Chapter 24

It was dusk when Marnie tried sneaking away from Lizette and Dane to give Nola a call and see what was up. She could hardly believe something warranted three 911-ish-type messages, but she wanted to make sure nobody had been maimed and rushed to the hospital.

Unfortunately Marnie would just have to keep wondering — the call went directly to Nola's voice mail, no rings or anything. She thought about hanging up and trying again later, but she glanced over to the swings where Dane was pushing Lizette, and decided to leave a message.

"Hey, Nol! Sorry I wasn't able to get ahold of you sooner but I was tied up playing touch football with Lizette and Dane and all those guys. It was such a blast! Anyway, we're probably going out for pizza or something, so I'll just catch up with you tomorrow during school, okay? And thanks again for your sweet gift! It's *soooooo* pretty! Bye!"

When Marnie hung up the phone, she felt a few pricks of guilt. If she loved Nola's bracelet so much, why had she let Lizette borrow it? And another thing: Lately Marnie had been telling Nola how much she missed her when she wasn't around, but Marnie had failed to say that on the phone just now. Did she *not* miss her? It didn't seem possible — two years ago, Marnie had suffered severe separation anxiety when Nola had gone to visit an aunt in Arkansas. Even last week, Marnie was sort of freaked about not having any classes with her. After last night, though, things felt different, and Marnie couldn't pinpoint exactly why.

She buttoned up her denim jacket and strolled toward the swings. Lizette jumped off one in midair and came crashing down in the dirt pit below her. She and Dane were laughing and smiling when Marnie jogged over, but Lizette was kind enough to excuse herself and go mingle with the rest of the crowd by the baseball field.

Dane took Marnie's hands in his and he brought her in close. She stood up on her tiptoes so that he wouldn't have to bend down far if he wanted to kiss her. He showed his appreciation by grinning, then running his bottom lip gently across her top lip. Marnie almost floated away.

Slowly he let go, but he made sure that one of his pinky fingers was touching hers. Then he gestured at the swing. "Wanna push?"

Within minutes, Marnie was flying higher than in any dream she'd ever had.

Marnie didn't get much sleep on Sunday night — she was up thinking about Dane until well after 11:30 — so she was dead tired on Monday morning. She wasn't even aware that Nola hadn't met her at the bus stop as usual, and when she got to her locker at school, she looked down and saw that she was wearing two different-colored thigh-high stockings (one navy blue and one black). It was obviously going to be one of those "off" days.

However, Marnie's mood began to brighten when she saw Nola getting her things together at her locker. She quickened her pace so she could catch her friend before homeroom and ask her if everything was all right, but Nola turned her back the second she saw her.

Here we go again.

Marnie steeled herself and tapped Nola on the shoulder. "Hi there."

Nola didn't respond. She just kept stacking her notebooks on top of a mammoth textbook as if Marnie weren't even there.

Marnie cleared her throat and tried again. "Nola, I said hi."

Nola kept rifling through her locker and pulled out a bag filled with pens, then started rifling through that.

"Are you *ignoring* me?" Marnie demanded, her voice shrill with anger.

How immature!

Nola pulled out a black pen and scribbled on a scrap sheet of paper to see if it was working. But Marnie's patience was running on an all-time low. She grabbed the pen out of Nola's hand and finally got her attention.

"What is your problem, Nola?" she shouted, a little louder than she'd intended to.

Nola threw Marnie a look of pure hostility. "Gee, I don't know. Why don't *you* tell me?"

Marnie clenched her fists. "What's that supposed to mean?"

"Well, there's got to be something wrong with *me* if you don't want to be my friend anymore." Nola slammed her locker door shut to emphasize just how angry she was.

Marnie felt herself turning furious. Why did Nola have to blow everything out of proportion? Just because Marnie had been a little less reliable lately and was getting to know new people didn't mean that she wanted to stop being friends with Nola. How come Nola couldn't understand? Was she *that* needy and territorial?

"That's not true and you know it," Marnie snapped. She could feel her body temperature rising and her ears especially felt hot.

Nola shoved her books into her tote bag and hurried down the hallway, keeping her head down.

Marnie chased after Nola. It was a knee-jerk reaction that she couldn't control. However, instead of consoling Nola when she caught up to her near homeroom 105, Marnie did something so out of the ordinary, it was practically unimaginable. She told her best friend off.

"You know what, Nola? I am *so* sick of your stupid attitude!" Marnie gnashed her teeth.

Nola didn't turn around. She just bolted into homeroom 105 and sat down at her desk, covering her face with her hands.

But Marnie couldn't scrounge up one shred of sympathy for her. When the bell rang, she elbowed through the crowded halls with brute force, hoping that Nola would stay far away from her.

At least for today.

Chapter 25

When Nola lifted her head and looked out the door, she saw that Marnie had left. She could feel her eyes tearing up, so she reached down into her bag and searched for some Kleenex. She had no luck — the only thing close to a tissue was a used wadded-up napkin from Stewart's, which Nola must have thrown into her bag during her last trip there with Marnie. The memory of that made her even weepier. Last week, she and Marnie had been as close as ever. Now everything had changed. Nola flattened the napkin out on her desk and then dabbed her eyes with it, hoping that no one would notice her crying.

But someone did.

"Are you okay?"

Nola glanced to her right and saw Matt sitting across from her, wearing a long-sleeved T-shirt and a pair of dark-brown cords. From the concerned look on his face, Nola could tell he was worried about her. She wanted nothing more than to give him a big hug, but she had the sense to restrain herself. Matt had a girlfriend, after all. After this morning, Nola wasn't sure if she should ever trust her own judgment again.

"No, I'm not," she replied.

"Wanna talk about it?" he asked.

"Not really."

Matt dug into his pants pocket and pulled out a pencil. He handed it to Nola and grinned. "If you tell me what's wrong, the pencil is yours."

Nola inspected it carefully and smiled despite herself. The pencil had the faces of the original members of KISS plastered all over it. "Really?"

"Yeah, I'd hate to part with it, but I hate seeing you sad even more."

This sweet comment made Nola want to cry harder.

"Marnie and I aren't getting along lately," Nola said, her voice wobbling.

"I see." Matt shifted in his seat so he could get a better look at Nola. "I'm sure whatever it is will blow over."

Nola wiped at her nose with the napkin. "Maybe."

"We haven't known each other very long, Nola, but over time, you'll see that . . . I'm always right," he joked, playfully kicking her leg.

Nola laughed. "Is that so?"

"'Tis very so." His smile was positively breathtaking.

All of a sudden, the sound of the door flying open echoed throughout the room. In walked Miss Lucas, looking more unkempt than ever before. Nola wondered if she should let her teacher know that her sweater was on inside-out, but when Miss Lucas collapsed in her chair and shouted, "Quiet (hiccup) everyone, or else you'll get (hiccup) the hose!" she decided not to.

Matt mouthed the words "Talk to you later" and turned toward the front of the classroom. Nola tried to regain her composure and opened up her notebook to do some mindless doodling with her new pencil. She'd drawn a couple of stick figures and some wavy lines along the border when she glanced up to see what time it was. Although homeroom was almost over, Nola had no idea that the beginning of the end was near until Lizette entered the room, late as usual.

For once, she wasn't wearing anything crazy — just a pair of skinny black pants and a black sleeveless turtle-neck sweater. The monochromatic outfit automatically directed Nola's attention to the colorful bracelet on Lizette's wrist.

A bracelet Nola was all too familiar with.

Nola swore she could feel every single muscle in her body clench tightly. *She. Is. Wearing. Marnie's. Bracelet!*

Nola bit on the pencil Matt gave her to stop herself from screaming at the top of her lungs.

"Nice of you (hiccup) to join us," Miss Lucas said to Lizette with a sneer. "One more tardy and I'm writing you up."

Lizette obviously saw how hypocritical Miss Lucas

was being, so she just rolled her eyes and sat down. "What*ever*."

Nola couldn't take her eyes off Lizette's wrist. Her thoughts were being processed at speeds that are oftentimes clocked at a racetrack. Why had Marnie given the bracelet to Lizette? How could Marnie be so callous and disrespectful? Didn't their friendship mean *anything* to her?

Soon all the questions gave way to sheer anger. Nola was biting on the pencil so hard, she could taste the graphite on her tongue. She was enraged that Marnie had taken something so precious as the gift Nola made with her own two hands — and treated it as if it was just some ordinary piece of jewelry that could be handed off to anyone.

Nola was so infuriated that when the bell rang, she shot up from her desk and dashed out of the room. She ignored Matt when he called out, "Hey, wait up!" and pushed through the throngs of students who were bustling about on the way to their first classes. Then she saw Marnie going through her locker. Nola didn't even bother to think about what she was going to say. Instead, she spoke straight from her broken heart.

"How could you?!" Nola shouted as she came up from behind Marnie.

Marnie was so startled that she dropped her protractor. "How could I what?"

Nola knew her skin was about to erupt in hives, but she couldn't care less. "How could you give the bracelet that I made you to Lizette?" she shouted.

Marnie's mouth hung open as if she'd gotten caught cheating on her PSATs. She stood there, silent, seemingly searching for words that would explain the situation. But Nola didn't want to wait.

"Answer me, Marnie! Why did you give Lizette the bracelet?"

"I didn't *give* it to her, I *lent* it to her," Marnie said tersely. "And will you stop shouting? You're embarrassing me."

Nola glanced around and saw that people were staring at her and Marnie as they walked by. She couldn't care less about this either. "Oh, I *know* I embarrass you. I've gotten that hint all the times you've hurt me in the last week!"

"What are you talking about?"

"Don't play dumb with me, Marnie. You've been ignoring me ever since you started hanging out with Lizette!"

Marnie squared her shoulders. "Well, maybe I did that because you were acting like *a big baby*! Would you just *grow up* already and stop being such a pain?!"

Nola was fuming. Marnie was telling *her* to grow up? "Please. At least I don't chase after Lizette and her friends like a pathetic little *wannabe.*"

Marnie shook her head as if she'd been decked in the jaw.

Nola glanced around again and noticed that an actual crowd had formed to watch their argument. Lizette, Grier, and Brynne weren't more than a few feet away. Even Matt was standing ringside, and still, she felt she couldn't back down. She was beyond angry. In fact, Nola almost felt like she hated Marnie.

"If you want to know what pathetic is, I'd suggest that you *look in the mirror!*" Marnie yelled in Nola's face.

"*Me* look in the mirror? That's pretty funny coming from the vainest, most conceited person I know!"

"Well maybe you should just forget you know me *at all!*"

Nola was just about to unleash all kinds of hurt on Marnie when Matt stepped between them. "Guys, don't make me get Miss Lucas and her hose. It won't be pretty."

Everyone in the crowd laughed, but Marnie stared at Nola, stone-faced. Nola stared back, breathing so hard she thought she might faint. She was wondering what Marnie was going to do next. Part of her hoped that she'd fall to her knees and beg for forgiveness, and the other part hoped this was some sort of night terror that she'd wake up from and everything would be as it was.

What she didn't expect was for Marnie to carefully close her locker door, spin around, cheerily link arms with Lizette, and walk away without another word, as if nothing had happened.

Nola could hear that Matt was saying something to her, but none of it was registering. There were only two thoughts being processed in her mind, which were repeating themselves over and over again like a skip in an mp3 file.

First, from now on, Marnie would be out of her life and in Lizette's circle of friends. And second, there would be no one around to love her like a sister.

Acknowledgments

Heartfelt thanks go out to my friend and editor Aimee Friedman, for her extraordinary editorial guidance and laughing at all of my jokes; Abigail McAden, for the chance to bring these characters to life; Priscilla Ma, for her willingness to push everything aside so that she could read early versions of the manuscript; my parents, Paul and Yvonne, and siblings, Luci and Paul Jacob, for their constant support and encouragement; my circle of friends (you know who you are), for getting me out of my apartment and away from my computer when I needed it most; and Bill Buchanan, for cheering me on.

Take a sneak peek at

LOVES ME, LOVES ME NOT
An IN or OUT novel

"Can I sit here?" A cheery, upbeat voice drifted into Nola's ear.

Slowly, Nola brought her face out from behind her hands and glanced up. Iris Santos was greeting her with a smirk and her signature head shake/bangs fling, which revealed her dark yet shining eyes.

Nola nodded her head and scooted over toward the window.

"Bad day, huh?" Iris said.

Nola sighed heavily. "You could say that again."

"Bad day, huh?" Now Iris's grin was of the size of Cheshire cat proportions. "Sorry! I couldn't resist."

Nola was in no mood for Iris's jokes. In fact, Nola wondered what Iris was doing on the bus in the first place. Usually Iris had debate team after school, and then her mom would pick her up. "How come you're not at practice?" Nola asked.

"Oh, Mrs. Wasserman flaked out because her husband got her tickets to see some sort of poor man's *Stars on Ice* show at the Civic Center." Iris rolled her eyes and crossed her arms over her chest defiantly. "The woman does *not* represent."

Nola could only manage a half-smile.

"But enough about me. How are you holding up, girl?"

"I'm . . . okay," Nola mumbled.

"Yeah. Right. And I'm soft-spoken and shy," Iris said with a snicker. "Listen, Marnie is going to realize how bogus those chicks are one day. She will."

Nola could tell that Iris was trying to make her feel better, but it wasn't working. Still, she was relieved she had someone to lean on if Marnie got on the bus, which could happen any second now.

All of a sudden, there was a TAP-TAP-TAP! on the glass.

Nola's breath caught in her throat.

She looked out the window and there stood Matt Heatherly. One of his hands was on the handlebar of his bike and the other one was in the air, waving hello. In an instant, Nola's emotions went from tortured to euphoric. He looked amazing. His hair was uncombed (as per usual), his faded jeans were falling down a little, and the cuffs on his beat-up Army jacket were rolled up, so she could see his blue wristband.

And in the next instant, Nola was thrown back to tortured status.

Riley Finnegan, she thought. *He has a girlfriend named Riley Finnegan.*

Iris stood up on the seat, leaned over Nola, and opened the window. "Whaddya want, peon?" she shouted.

"You still mad about the other day?" Matt smiled, and then broke into a laugh. "I'm sorry our date was a wash, okay? I'm afraid I'm taken."

Nola's stomach churned so hard she thought she might double over in pain.

"That is one *desperate* female," Iris said, tossing her hair with attitude.

Matt shook his head. "Iris, just tell Nola to come out here."

"Tell her yourself!" And with that, Iris slammed the window shut and sat back down.

Nola saw Matt smirking at her and she couldn't help

but give a half-smile back. He gestured with his head, beckoning her to meet him outside. Nola looked back at Iris, who was chuckling to herself.

"By all means, Nola." Iris got up and cleared a path for her.

"Thanks." Nola grabbed her things and made her way down the aisle. As she descended the steps, Matt rolled his bike over to welcome her.

"Hey," he said.

Nola swallowed hard. "Hey."

"I wanted to know if you needed a lift home."

"Um, Matt, in case you didn't notice, I was on *the bus*," she pointed out.

Matt scratched his head. "Yeah, good point."

Nola knew what he was up to, though. He was checking on her to see if she was okay. How sweet was *that*?

"Still, the bus is so . . . old school, don't you think? Wouldn't you rather see the greater Poughkeepsie region on the seat of a bike, driven by a retired paperboy?" Matt patted the vinyl seat with his hands.

Nola's horrible day was fading slowly from her thoughts. So much so, that she found it easy to actually tease Matt. "I think I'd rather live to see fourteen."

"I turned fourteen over the summer. Don't believe the hype," he said, grinning.

Nola laughed. Everything was easy with him. *Everything*.

"Come on, you know you want to," Matt teased. "And this is a one-time offer. You snooze, you lose."

Nola could hardly argue with him. She did want to sit on that bike and hold onto Matt's waist for dear life. She did want him to give her an escape route — the bus was going to leave soon and Marnie was sure to come dashing out of the back doors to where the buses were lined up for departure. She did want him to make her forget about her terrible day and all the terrible days that were to come. But more than anything, Nola wanted to forget that Riley Finnegan ever existed. Then it dawned on her that if she accepted this bike ride, maybe, possibly, Matt might forget Riley existed, too.

"Just don't pull any crazy stunts, all right?" Nola said as she approached him cautiously.

Matt took his free hand and patted her gently on the back. "I promise, Nola, I would never do anything to hurt you."

When Matt pedaled off with Nola holding his waist and her legs dangling off the sides, she asked herself if she could ever believe in promises again.

She would have to wait and see.

stamen

pistil

ovary

ovules